A Horse of HER OWN

A Horse

OF HER OWN

by Selma Hudnut

Illustrated by *Rus Anderson*

WILDSIDE PRESS

TO

THE LOS ALTOS HUNT

may they long enjoy good hunting!

CONTENTS

1. *"I Wouldn't Have It Any Other Way"*

Rosemary was an audience of one in a front-row seat. She wrapped her worn tan coat around her thin legs and settled herself under the apricot tree. Beyond that, she ignored the sharp February wind. The only bright moments of the dull routine of her day were beginning.

In the riding ring just below her at the bottom of the hill, a man was riding a brown horse. She was pretty sure he didn't know she was there and, unless she accidentally sent dirt clods rolling, he wouldn't have any reason to look up in her direction.

The muffled sound of a telephone reached her. It came from the house which she could see by shifting her eyes to the left. From her seat in the orchard, the whole panorama of the man's property was spread out below her.

There was a barn beyond the ring, a parking space for cars, and a driveway leading to the garage beside the house. She could even see a path from the driveway dropping down to the front door.

The phone rang distantly again but the rider didn't hear. His attention was on his horse. He was being patient but knew exactly what he wanted. The horse was either young, or green, or both. Rosemary thought he probably understood what the man was asking him to do but didn't want to trot and canter in such a restrained way. The horse was wet with sweat and steaming in the cold air.

"Jonathan! Oh, Jonathan! You're wanted on the phone." A woman had come to the front door of the house. She had to call again before he heard her.

"Who is it?" he shouted. "I can't come to the phone now. Can't you take a message?"

"You'll *have* to come, Jonathan! It's Mr. Fuller. He says it's too complicated to explain to me. He says he has to talk to *you*."

"Well—you'll have to walk Understudy for me. He's too hot to put in his stall."

"I'm sorry, dear. I have something in the oven I can't leave. OHHHH!" she finished in a wail and disappeared in the house.

Before the conversation had ended, Rosemary was standing at the fence that separated the orchard from the man's driveway. He saw her just as she opened her mouth to speak.

2

"Say—do you know anything at all about horses? Could you walk this one around the ring for me while I answer the phone? He won't give you any trouble and I'll only be a few minutes."

Rosemary nodded as she put her canvas sneaker expertly on the bottom strand of the barbed-wire fence. Pulling the middle and top strands of the wire together with her fingers, she was through the fence safely in one quick motion.

She jumped down the last bit of hill to the driveway below and stooped to go through the panel fence encircling the ring.

"I'll be happy to walk him for you," she said as she reached for the reins.

"You're not afraid of horses, are you?" he asked and as she shook her head, he continued, "Understudy likes to be walked—it's only when you're on his back that he tries to argue with you," he finished with a smile.

Rosemary smiled back at him. When he had started down the path to his front door, she let out her breath in a long sigh of satisfaction. She stroked the horse on his neck, not caring that it made her hand wet and sticky.

This was the first horse she'd been near since she'd moved to Las Parra from Berkeley with her Uncle Ed, her cousins, and her uncle's new wife, right after the Christmas holidays.

She felt like pinching herself to make sure she wasn't dreaming! She'd begun to think she'd have to learn to live without horses, just as she'd had to learn to live without her parents this last year or more.

As far back as she could remember in her thirteen years, there had been horses. Her father always had a horse or two of his own at the smaller race tracks in California and could always get jobs training and running outside horses for their owners.

Then her Aunt Maureen, her mother's sister and Uncle Ed's wife, had come to the Santa Rosalia County Fair to visit them. She had wanted to buy a present for her sister's birthday. Rosemary's mother had decided she wanted to do some shopping, too, and at the last moment her father went with them. He'd wanted a special feed for a horse he was training that wasn't eating properly. That was how it happened that they'd gone in Aunt Maureen's car. And none of them had come back.

Rosemary had been grateful to Uncle Ed for taking her into his home. She suspected that he had felt responsible for his wife's niece. Besides, she had no place else to go. Her mother had had no other relatives and her father's family—a younger brother, married and with children—was in Ireland.

Uncle Ed had never exactly said what her duties were to be but she'd fallen into the routine of running the house.

Her cousins, Bruce, older than she, and Joseph, two years younger, had quickly adjusted to the loss of their mother. As long as meals were ready when they were hungry and they had clean clothes where they could find them, they were content in the little time they spent at home. Their interests changed with the seasons—from marbles, yo-yos, and kites for Joe, to baseball, swimming, and football for Bruce.

Uncle Ed brought the food home and took the soiled clothes to the launderette. Rosemary did the rest.

She never lost a gnawing ache of loneliness but, after

4

she discovered a riding stable in the Berkeley hills, she spent every free moment there. When she was with horses, in an odd kind of way, she felt as though she were with part of her family.

She'd worked at the stables her whole summer vacation. She fed and watered, helped to clean stalls, saddled and bridled the rent horses for classes and even taught.

When Uncle Ed abruptly married again and moved to Las Parra, Rosemary suffered another loss at having to leave the riding stable.

She shook her head to forget the unhappy past. Right now she was walking a handsome thoroughbred gelding named Understudy.

She felt the stirrup iron behind her, swaying back and forth with every stride the horse took. The owner was so tall, the irons dangled almost below the horse's girth. She stopped and automatically picked up the iron in her right hand. With her left, she held the leather and slid the iron up under the flap of the saddle where the buckle rested. At the same time, she ran the stirrup leather through the iron to secure it and did the same on the other side. "There—that looks neater," she said, and resumed her walk.

"I can't thank you enough." The horse's owner was back, smiling as he spoke.

Rosemary was startled. She'd almost forgotten him. For a few moments she could have been walking a horse anywhere—even at a race track with her parents close by.

He looked at Rosemary and then his glance went back to the saddle, with the iron tucked under the flap, and his eyes widened in surprise.

"Do you ride?" he asked.

"Yes, I do."

"Would you like to ride Understudy and finish cooling him out? He's still warm. You'd be doing me a favor because I have another horse to work."

"Oh, I'd love to." Rosemary was already starting to shorten a stirrup. Luckily she was wearing jeans.

"I guess we'd better introduce ourselves," the man said as he adjusted the leather on the other side for her. "My name's Jonathan Sedgwick."

"How do you do? I'm Rosemary O'Connor."

"Do you live around here, Rosemary? It seems to me I've heard about a new family over the hill."

"Yes, I guess that's us. Do you have a daughter named Cindy? I think she's in my class at school."

"I certainly do. And she's never around when I need her. I wish she were as interested in horses as you are. As a matter of fact, I'd settle for having her one-half as interested. Well—no matter now. I'll join you as soon as I have Sea saddled."

"C saddled?"

"It's spelled S-e-a. Silver Sea. Not A-B-C."

Rosemary rode Understudy around the ring, trying to imagine what his gaits would be like at a trot and a canter, savoring every moment of sitting on a horse's back. All the loneliness of the last few months faded— when she'd felt like a stranger in her uncle's house with his new wife there—when she'd felt like a stranger at school, where it was so hard to get acquainted.

Mr. Sedgwick must love horses as much as she did— and as her father had done and his father before him —in Ireland.

Why, when her father was her age, he was hacking

6

ladies' hunters to a meet side-saddle. Ah, it made her smile to think of her father as a curly-headed boy riding an Irish hunter side-saddle!

Mr. Sedgwick returned to the ring leading a flea-bitten gray gelding with powerful quarters, sturdy legs, and wise eyes. Wise, old eyes, she thought, if the hollows above them meant anything.

She was careful not to get in Mr. Sedgwick's way as he worked the gray. Sea felt good. He squealed when he started out and gave a few buck jumps. This caused Understudy to start skittering across the ring. Rosemary quickly brought him back to the track and settled him down.

"Good girl," Mr. Sedgwick said. "You must have had a lot of experience with horses."

"All my life—but not since we moved to Las Parra." She looked beyond the trees and hills and continued, "I have a picture someone took of me when I was a year old. My father had one of those saddles that look like a wicker basket. He used to strap me in it and pony my horse off his."

"Your father had the right idea," Mr. Sedgwick nodded his head. "I should have started with Cindy when she was a year old. But I don't have too much time to spend with horses. I thought it was better psychology to wait until *she* wanted to ride and *she* asked me to teach her. Well . . ." he finished ruefully, "I waited too long."

He went back to working his horse. When he was through, he brought Sea down to a walk and waited for Rosemary to catch up. He seemed to be studying her position in the saddle. Finally he said, "You didn't get much of a ride today just cooling him out. I'd like both of the horses to have a good work-out tomorrow. Would you like to ride with me? You could have Sea. Understudy needs more schooling before he's a 'lady's mount.' "

"I'd l . . . love to," she said, so pleased she stuttered. "What time?"

"About the same as today."

They continued to walk their horses together. Mr. Sedgwick was clever at asking simple little questions. Before she knew it, she was telling him about her mother and father and the accident. And then, of her own accord, she told him about living in Berkeley with her uncle and working at the riding stables.

A girl, about Rosemary's age, came up the driveway on a bicycle. She called, "Hi, Dad," and started towards the garage.

"Cindy, come over here a minute," her father directed. He stopped his horse and motioned Rosemary to do the same.

"This is my daughter, Cindy, and this is Rosemary O'Connor. You two girls should know each other. Rosemary tell me she's in your class. She's a new-comer to Las Parra and almost our next-door neighbor. She lives just over the hill."

"Hi," Cindy said. "I thought I remembered you from school."

Rosemary looked at her admiringly. They were about the same height, but Cindy was all soft curves. Her hair was short and blonde, cut with feathery edges. She was dressed in a plaid skirt and a light blue cashmere sweater with long sleeves. Charm bracelets dangled from her arm.

That's the kind of clothes I'll probably never in my life be able to have, Rosemary thought with a sigh. Everything Cindy wore would have to make frequent trips to the dry cleaners. Even her white buckskin shoes looked impractical—impractical but wonderful. Rosemary's clothes had to be the kind that could be thrown into the washing machine.

Aloud she said, "Hello, Cindy. You're about the first girl I've had a chance to talk to since we came here."

Mr. Sedgwick raised his eyebrows but didn't say anything. Presently Cindy said, "Well, see you at school," and got back on her bicycle.

Her father seemed to be trying to apologize. "You know, Cindy not only isn't interested in horses, I think she actively dislikes them. She thinks people who like horses are slightly crazy. Well . . . maybe we are, but I wouldn't have it any other way, would you?"

"I should say not," said Rosemary, looking down at the reins she was holding. "I should say not," she repeated softly, as her fingers gently closed on the reins.

2. *Tally-ho!*

As soon as she got home, Rosemary headed for the shed behind Uncle Ed's house. Her father's trunks had been stored there until it was decided what to do with them. She hadn't liked the idea of keeping the tack and her riding clothes in an old shed, over-run with mice, but her new aunt didn't want them cluttering up the house.

Rosemary knew just where to look for her things. She found jodhpurs, shoes, and a worn riding coat with suede patches on the elbows in the smallest trunk. It wasn't really a trunk—it was a tackbox from the stable.

She'd hang up the jacket and jodhpurs, she decided, to get rid of the smell of moth balls. Later, she could

10

press them. Then Mr. Sedgwick wouldn't be ashamed of her. She'd been lucky today to have worn jeans. She couldn't have ridden otherwise; but she'd noticed that Mr. Sedgwick had on jodhpurs and a tweed coat.

She carried the clothes to her room, off the enclosed back porch, and found hangers. Then she went to help with dinner.

She didn't mind too much that Cindy didn't talk to her at school next day. She wasn't too sure she'd expected her to be friendly. Rosemary knew she didn't fit into the pattern set by the girls in her class.

They all had short, pixie hair cuts—like Cindy's— or pony tails, and she still arranged her curly black hair in the braids her father had liked so well.

Her dresses were too long to be fashionable. They were so old and faded, she didn't see any point in shortening them. If she'd only grow a little, she thought with a sigh, it would save her the trouble, anyway. Uncle Ed's friend who had shopped for Rosemary believed in getting dresses with plenty of room for growing. She hadn't grown very much and now the dresses were wearing out and still didn't fit.

She knew she was too thin and too pale. She was so white her freckles showed up worse than ever. Her father always said she had beautiful blue eyes with their thick, tangled eyelashes. He was the only one, though, who had ever admired them. Oh, well, she thought, it didn't matter what your face looked like when you were riding.

Just before she set out for the Sedgwick house next day, she polished her jodhpur shoes, thankful they still fit. Taking the short-cut through the orchard got them

11

dusty, so she wiped each shoe carefully on the back of her legs. Then she reached back to brush off her jodhpurs with her hand and went through the barbed-wire fence.

Mr. Sedgwick was already in the barn, taking Sea out of his stall. He crosstied him and reached for a brush.

"Let me do that," Rosemary said eagerly. "We can each work on one, can't we?"

He laughed. "We sure can! But most of my guests like to have their horses saddled and ready for them. You're rapidly becoming my favorite rider."

He put a saddle on Sea and then handed her a snaffle bridle. He watched her put it on, nodding approval at the way she managed. When Understudy was ready, they walked their horses out of the barn to mount.

Leaving the pavement, they rode through fields, passing from one to another through gates hardly noticeable. They walked up and down hills and trotted in the flat places.

"We're going to Alec Randolph's place to school Understudy on some outside jumps," Mr. Sedgwick explained. "I want to take him out hunting on Saturday and he's still pretty green."

"You mean there's a hunt around here? Really?" Rosemary asked in surprise.

"There certainly is." Mr. Sedgwick sounded proud. "It's a drag hunt because there are no foxes in California and we go out every Wednesday and Saturday from October to February. The hunt was started a few years ago. I was one of the charter members. You know —there are only two others in California." He was launched on what was obviously one of his favorite subjects.

When they arrived at the Randolph place, he explained that none of the family was home but that he had permission to use the jumps. "As a matter of fact, everyone has a standing invitation to come over and school," he said.

The course extended through a large field in front of the house and a wooded area with a creek running through it beside the house. A wire fence separated the two sections and was panelled in a number of places. The jumps were all permanent and of solid construction.

This was the first outside course Rosemary had ever seen other than the one in the infield of the race track at the State Fair Grounds. This was different, though, more natural looking and informal and much bigger, she thought.

Mr. Sedgwick told her where to take Sea, so she could have the best view of the jumps. "I might as well do it all while I'm about it," he said.

She sat on the gray at the top of a knoll, with an uninterrupted view, not only of the course, but of the hills and valleys beyond. She patted Sea's neck. If Mr. Sedgwick weren't so close by, she'd have thrown her arms around the gelding. This was a lot more fun than huddling under a tree in the orchard to watch him ride his horse in the ring.

He was galloping Understudy now in a large circle and then urged him on to a stone wall with a rail over it. The brown horse took off way back and cleared the jump by a good foot and galloped on to the next one,

13

clearly eager to go faster. Mr. Sedgwick checked him but the gelding didn't want to slow down. He tossed his head and fretted for more rein. On the next jump he got in too close but managed to clear it handily. Then he settled down and jumped in good style.

Rosemary could see the effects of the ring work the brown horse had been given. Schooling made horses more responsive to their riders' wishes, handier and safer, and here was the proof.

When he rode back, she said, "That looked like fun. Understudy settled down real well, didn't he?"

"Yes, he did. I'm very pleased with the way he's going. Do you jump, Rosemary?"

She nodded—absolutely speechless.

"Would you like to do the course—or part of it? Sea will take good care of you."

She finally found her tongue. "I haven't jumped for a long time. I did help school horses in Berkeley, but they weren't very good ones," she finished candidly.

He nodded, as though he understood about rent horses. "Suppose you try those two jumps over there first and see how you get along," and he indicated the ones he meant. "Then you can come back over here," and he pointed to the jump where he had started, "and do the whole thing."

Rosemary walked Sea down the knoll, began to trot on the flat, and put him into a canter in a large circle in exact imitation of Mr. Sedgwick.

She could almost hear her father's voice, "Keep your heels down and your head up, lass, and throw your heart over the jump first."

14

As soon as Sea took off for the first fence, she knew that Mr. Sedgwick was right. Sea would take care of her. She came off the second jump and slowed down to start the course at the point Mr. Sedgwick had suggested. She looked at him questioningly.

"Perfect! Sea's jumping as well as I've ever seen him. He's probably happy not to have to pack my weight over the jumps."

Rosemary galloped Sea to the stone wall with the rail on top, hoping he would continue to be happy. He seemed to measure his distance to the jumps and arrive at each one with mathematical precision. He didn't have to take off too far back to jump, nor get in too close.

It was easy to follow the course. There was enough room between jumps to look around and find the next one. Besides, Sea had undoubtedly jumped here before and knew where to go.

She jumped the panel into the next field, galloped through the trees, and saw the path turn towards the creek. She made the turn, slowed Sea down, and saw a drop straight down to the creek and up a steep bank on the other side. She urged the gray down the bank, walked him through the water which came up almost to his knees, and he scrambled up the other side.

Back on the flat ground, Sea started galloping of his own accord. Rosemary let out a delighted whoop and shouted, "Tally-ho!" She didn't know what it meant—it had something to do with hunting, she thought—but it sounded good. "Tally-ho!" she shouted again, as she saw a rustic post and rail jump some distance in front of her.

15

"Tally-ho to you, too," came from the trees to her left.

She was so startled she almost dropped her reins. Sea faltered in his stride and she steadied him hastily and brought him down to a walk. Then, in a flush of embarrassment, she looked toward the voice.

A sandy-haired boy, a year or two older than she, was sitting relaxed on a beautiful brown mare, dappled and fine. Rosemary couldn't bear to look beyond the mare's ears. He must think she was crazy, yelling like that.

"I didn't mean to spoil your fun but I was afraid Sea would spook at us when you turned around and came back. Is Jonathan schooling his green horse?"

She nodded. At least he didn't think she was crazy. Not if he was willing to ask a sensible question and expect to get a sensible answer.

"Go ahead and finish the course. You looked like you were having fun; I think I'll jump the rest of it behind you. Then I can say 'hello' to Jonathan. By the way, my name's Pete Hughes."

"My name is Rosemary O'Connor."

"Do you belong to the hunt?" he asked with interest. "If you don't, I'll bet Jonathan is working on you. He never lets a good rider get away."

"No, I don't," she said. "I didn't even know there was such a thing until today. We've just moved here." She didn't know what was possessing her! To answer this boy as though all she needed to join the hunt was to make up her mind. But why tell him all the unpleasant details? He wouldn't want to hear them. Her honesty made her add, "I don't have a horse to ride anyway."

"Well, Saturday's the last hunt of the season. Maybe

16

by next fall you'll have a horse. Anyone who likes to ride as much as you should have one."

"I think so, too," she said, "but Mr. Sedgwick will think I've had an accident if I don't get back pretty quick." With that she gathered up the reins and Sea broke into a canter.

After the post and rail there was an oxer to jump, then back through the trees and over an in-and-out, down into the creek at a different point and up the bank to join the original path she'd followed.

Rosemary looked back and saw Pete leaning forward in his saddle as his mare galloped up to the jump Sea had just taken. He grinned and called, "Tally-ho!" as the mare sailed over the jump.

"Tally-ho," Rosemary answered sheepishly.

When they came in sight of the finish of the course, Pete shouted, "Wait for me and we'll jump in pairs. The fences are wide enough."

Rosemary slowed Sea's gait down to a canter. Pete put on a burst of speed. Just before he reached her, she squeezed her legs. The gray gelding responded as though he knew exactly what they had in mind. They went over the last two jumps in perfectly matched strides, the two horses taking off at the same time, landing on the far side together and finishing as one.

"Bravo!" Mr. Sedgwick called to them. "We'll have to think about making up a team for the hunter trials. Hello, Pete. I'm glad to see you two are acquainted.

"Did Pete hold you up, Rosemary? I was beginning to think you'd gotten into trouble. I shouldn't have worried, though. You gave Sea one of the best rides he's ever had."

17

"Oh, thank you," she said. "That's because he's so willing. Did you train him, too?"

"Yes, I did. He was my first horse."

"Rosemary says she doesn't belong to the hunt," Pete interrupted. "Don't you think we ought to do something about it?"

"Yes, we should. But Saturday is the last hunt of the season and a friend of mine, who's becoming very interested in joining, is going to ride Sea.

"If you'd like to hack the gray to the place where the hunt starts, Rosemary, I'll see that you get a ride in a car and watch it on foot. That's *almost* as exciting as riding in it."

"Oh, yes, I'd love to," Rosemary answered eagerly.

Pete said he had to get home, he had studying to do. After saying good-bye to Mr. Sedgwick, he turned to Rosemary and with a grin raised his hand in salute and said, "Tally-ho, Rosie! See you Saturday."

"We'd better get along, too," Mr. Sedgwick said. "This wind is cold and the horses shouldn't stand. How would you like some hot chocolate when we get back?"

"Sounds wonderful," she answered, beginning to get cold herself now that the excitement of the jumping was over.

"Which do you prefer being called—Rosemary or Rosie?" Mr. Sedgwick asked as they walked their horses down the road.

Rosemary could feel her cheeks getting warm. "It doesn't really matter."

"Rosemary is such a pretty name. I think I'll stick to that and leave Rosie for Pete."

18

Rosemary or Rosie—which did she prefer? Her father had named her Rosemary Margaret Ann Teresa O'Connor. Her mother always said he'd run out of breath or she would have had more names. Sometimes her mother added that her father tried to invoke the aid of all the saints on Rosie!

Rosie! She was called that now by her uncle and Bruce and Joe, and even by her uncle's new wife. But it didn't sound the same as when her father had called her Rosie.

Sometimes, before she went to bed, he had told her stories of Ireland—of horses and hunting and showing. She remembered names like The Meath and the Scarteen Black and Tan's and Limerick and Tipperary.

Then he'd call her by her full name, softly—"Rosemary Margaret Ann Teresa O'Connor," give her a hug and say, "Off to bed, Rosie-Posie. Good night, Posie." No one had ever called her Posie except her father. And he only called her that when they were alone.

Never again would she hear someone call her Posie in that sweet, teasing Irish way and never again would she hear someone call her Rosemary Margaret Ann Teresa O'Connor. For she never told anyone her full name. . . .

After the horses were put away, Mr. Sedgwick and Rosemary went into the house which she had seen so many times from the orchard above. She was introduced to Mrs. Sedgwick, who was very pretty and young-looking close up, and who made her feel welcome.

Mrs. Sedgwick showed her where to wash her hands and then told her to make herself comfortable in the living room. She sat close to the crackling fire and

19

hoped the Sedgwicks would be a long time. There was so much to look at.

Hunting prints decorated the white adobe brick walls; the very sofa on which she sat was slip-covered with a heavy linen print of horses and hounds. The mantelpiece overflowed with figures of horses. On the credenza was a huge, ornate silver bowl, won by Silver Sea, according to the engraving.

What a darling house, she thought. She'd never seen anything so cozy—so comfortable. Books and magazines spilled over everywhere. Mrs. Sedgwick's influence could be seen in the arrangement of leaves and berries, the shelves in the windows with vases and bottles of colored glass to catch the sun and sparkle back. Cindy was the luckiest girl in the world to have such a home and family and *horses!*

She tried to memorize every detail of the room so she could think about it later. Someday, maybe, she could have one exactly like it.

All too soon Mr. Sedgwick returned, carrying a large silver tray holding cups and saucers, napkins and a heaping plate of cookies. Mrs. Sedgwick joined them with a silver pot from which she poured the steaming chocolate.

"We had a good school, didn't we, Rosemary?" Mr. Sedgwick asked, relaxing by the fireplace, his long legs stretched out in front of him. "I think Understudy will get along all right on Saturday."

He addressed his wife. "Rosemary is the best find I've ever made. She can do anything on a horse—hack, jump, exercise. AND, she insists on taking care of her own horse!

20

"You know, the older I get, the less enthusiasm I have for cuffing off horses and putting saddles on and taking them off."

Rosemary could feel her cheeks getting warm and it wasn't because of the mouthful of hot chocolate she'd swallowed. She was relieved when Cindy walked into the living room from outdoors.

"Hi," Cindy greeted them.

"You're not just getting home from school, are you?" her father asked.

"Oh, no. I've been home and gone out again. Gosh, it's cold outside. May I have some hot chocolate, Mother?"

"Of course, dear. Bring a cup."

"We rode over to the Randolphs' today," Mr. Sedgwick explained for his daughter's benefit when she returned from the kitchen. "I wanted to give Understudy a last school before the hunt tomorrow. We met Pete Hughes."

Cindy looked up with interest. "What was he doing?"

"Riding his mare. He and Rosemary met somewhere on the outside course and they wound up by giving a nice exhibition of pair jumping.

"Would you like to go in Hunt Teams with us at the Las Parra Hunter Trials, Rosemary? Two brown horses and a gray won't look too bad."

"Oh, yes," she answered quickly.

"Good, that's a date then." A thought seemed to strike him suddenly. "You know, it's a funny thing about Pete. I think you've made a conquest, Rosemary. He usually doesn't bother with girls—not even the ones who ride."

21

Rosemary could feel herself blushing again and glanced down at her cup, rattling in its saucer. When her hand steadied, she looked up and her gaze fell on Cindy, glaring at her!

3. The Hunt

Rosemary woke up much too early the morning of the hunt. She knew it as soon as she looked out the window. Not the faintest streak of light showed in the sky. She was positive she'd never get to sleep again. She might as well get dressed as lie in bed, shivering in anticipation.

She hoped she'd look all right. Even though she wasn't going to ride in the hunt—she'd be with people who were. A clean white shirt, a neat bow tie her uncle had loaned her, and a tweed coat with patched elbows were all she had. Well, she'd have to make the best of it.

She tiptoed to the kitchen so she wouldn't awaken

the rest of the family and quietly fixed herself some hot chocolate and toast for breakfast. She wasn't very hungry but it gave her something to do.

When she couldn't bear dawdling over the half-cold chocolate any longer, she carried her dishes to the sink and rinsed them. Then, since it was still early, she walked on the road, the long way, to the Sedgwick house.

At the barn, the horses were saddled and bridled and tied up. Rosemary was petting Sea on his velvety, inquisitive nose when Mr. Sedgwick's cheery voice boomed through the barn.

"Good morning. Are you all set?"

He looked as though he'd stepped out of a hunting print, Rosemary thought, in scarlet coat, immaculate white breeches, and black boots with tan cuffs. In his hand he held a velvet hunting cap and hunting whip.

"Good morning," she answered. "I wish I'd thought —I could have been here earlier and braided the horses."

"Now, *that* would have been a treat!" he said. "We almost never braid. I used to," he continued, musing, "but that's another one of the things you skip when it gets to be too much of an effort. Now, if I had a stableman to do it for me . . ."

As they hacked down the road, Mr. Sedgwick explained, "If the hunt meet is far away, I take my horse in the trailer, of course. But it's only a fifteen- or twenty-minute ride today and I think Understudy can use the work."

He talked about the hunt and his responsibilities as Field Master. It was his job, he said, to see that the field, meaning the riders, didn't let their horses get out of hand and over-ride hounds, didn't bunch up at jumps, and didn't get into trouble.

It seemed to Rosemary that in no time at all they turned into a narrow road deep in perpetual shade from towering redwoods, squat madrones and maple trees. In a clearing, she saw trailers and horses—men, women, and children. As the riders adjusted their tack and checked bridles, they called out greetings to newcomers and exchanged news.

Mr. Sedgwick said, "Good morning, Mrs. Hopkins," to a woman who had greeted him. Then he asked, "Are you going to watch the hunt?"

"Yes, Bob and I are," she answered, nodding at a teenage boy standing by a white convertible nearby.

After introducing Rosemary, Mr. Sedgwick explained that she wanted to watch the hunt and needed transportation. Mrs. Hopkins said she'd be happy to take her. She was nice and friendly, Rosemary decided, and looked awfully pretty in an oatmeal-colored sweater and skirt.

Mrs. Hopkins introduced her son, who told Rosemary he was on foot because his older sister, home from college for the week-end, was using his horse.

Mr. Sedgwick found his friend, who was going to hunt for the first time. Rosemary dismounted and relinquished Sea's reins.

"Next season you'll ride with us, Rosemary," Mr. Sedgwick promised.

She nodded and smiled at him but didn't say anything. She stood alone, out of the way of the horses, and yet not really alone. Everyone smiled and nodded

25

a greeting. She was completely bewitched at the sight of a lady, riding a typy gray horse side-saddle. She could hardly take her eyes off her.

The snatches of conversation she heard were fascinating—"I could cry when I realize this is the last hunt of the season. . . ."

"Brad wanted me to try out his new horse. I never saw it before this morning. . . ."

"Oh! This wretched beast won't stand still a minute. . . ."

"Mother couldn't find enough hunting caps to fit. Look at what David had to wear. He's furious. . . ."

Rosemary looked in the direction in which the girl was pointing and saw a boy with a hunting cap that rested at least three inches above his ears, held on by an elastic band.

She turned away to hide her smile, although she was sure no one was looking at her, and found herself face to face with Pete. He was wearing a scarlet coat and looked dignified and almost as old as Mr. Sedgwick until he grinned and said, "Good morning, Rosie! I'm glad you could make it. Next fall you'd better have a horse and come with us."

"I'll try," Rosemary said fervently. By some miracle, she thought, maybe by next fall she would have a horse and ride in the hunt. It would take a miracle—but just think—a week ago she hadn't known the hunt existed. Now here she was about to watch it.

What had been confusion and aimless wandering back and forth a moment before changed to orderly progress as the riders, by some unspoken signal, headed up a hill. Pete waved good-bye and joined two other boys. Mrs.

Hopkins called and Rosemary went to the car, her heart beginning to pound. The hunt was about to start.

Mrs. Hopkins and Bob were awfully good-natured as well as friendly, Rosemary decided. They didn't mind how many questions she asked and didn't even seem to mind answering the same ones over again. In her excitement, she found herself asking a question and then barely listening to the answer.

Mrs. Hopkins parked her car on the side of the road where other spectators had already gathered. Horses and hounds had reached a shallow valley, heavily wooded with scrub oak and baccaris. Buckeyes and maples hinted of a creek close by and the soft rose-red of the smooth madrone bark might have been put there to match the pink coats of the hunt staff and the riders qualified to wear them.

Horses galloped up a steep hill singly, hounds leading the way. Shivers went up and down Rosemary's spine and the palms of her hands were wet. Half-remembered phrases and incidents from the past, when her father had told her of Irish hunts, came to mind.

She could almost feel the pull on the reins as the eager horses fretted to be off. The excitement of anticipation would make them break out in a sweat; they would prance in resentment of the check in which they were held. The young ones would paw the ground nervously and tossing heads would blow a shower of foam.

Did she really hear the roan mare squeal in protest at not being allowed to start soon enough? She could almost believe the pungent smell of sweating hides filled her nostrils.

27

Her teeth chattered as she watched the pack stream over a rustic jump filled with brush at the top of the hill. Scarlet-coated riders followed. The hounds announced they were on the line. She could still hear the huntsman's "Gone awayyyy!"

Rosemary gave a long sigh of regret to see the last horse pulling to catch up with the field in front. Mrs. Hopkins waited until a small group of riders, escorted by a man in scarlet coat, went around the jump at a sedate gait.

"Those are the 'Hill Toppers,' " she explained. "They don't jump and they aren't up to going as fast as the people in the hunt. So they follow along at the end at a slower pace. The man riding the stock saddle on the palomino is my husband. It's a good way for him to get his horse exercised," she said, half-apologetically.

"Well, let's get back to the car and pick up the hunt again."

Bob went ahead and held the car door open for Rosemary. She was so surprised she stopped short. Like a spooky filly, she decided later, blushing as she thought of it. Imagine either one of her cousins ever holding a door open for a girl! When they opened a door—they went through it!

The spectators caught up with the hunt again when it was forced to slow down for a gate, walk down a narrow paved road, turn sharp, and, without any kind of a run, jump a three-foot chicken coop.

No two horses jumped it alike, Rosemary noticed. It was a good test for a handy hunter. The knowing horses crouched on their hocks, gave a mighty thrust, and were over the jump almost from a stand-still. The horses that

28

jumped off their forehand got into trouble. There were refusals, hard raps, and sticky jumps. One rider went over his horse's head and landed on his feet beyond the jump, still holding his reins and looking bewildered.

Pete waved to her as his mare trotted two strides and with effortless grace jumped and galloped on. The "Hill Toppers" found a gate to go through and once again Mrs. Hopkins said it was time to move on. Bob said he thought there would be one more place from which to observe the hunt.

"Oh, no!" Rosemary protested. "It *can't* be over so soon!"

Mrs. Hopkins said that the hunt, being laid in this particular area, unfortunately had to be a little short.

If this was her last chance, Rosemary thought, she wasn't going to miss a minute of it. She stared fixedly at the place where the hounds should appear, according to Bob.

A few moments before they had seen a man in frontier pants and a windbreaker, riding a compact, liver-chestnut horse. In a rocking-chair canter, he had taken his horse across the side of the hill, over a jump, and vanished in some scrub oaks.

Mrs. Hopkins explained that California had no foxes for the hounds to hunt; consequently, Charlie, the man they saw, was "laying the drag." He went ahead of the hunt, hauling a sack drenched with something that gave off a musk odor, the scent of which the hounds would follow. When he thought it time for a "check point," which was simply a rest period for horses, he lifted the sack so that the scent was lost temporarily and put it down some distance away.

"But does the same person have the job all the time?" Rosemary asked. "Wouldn't he rather hunt?"

"Yes, but the job is rotated among the people who are qualified to do it. Everyone has to take a turn."

They watched two young boys riding Western saddles, jog-trotting behind the drag man.

"I hope they don't ride over the scent," Mrs. Hopkins sounded worried. "If they do, they'll spoil it for the hounds. I think it's all right—their horses are travelling higher up the hill than Charlie did."

Rosemary, tired of straining her eyes toward the farthest hill, glanced at the pasture in front of her for the first time. She was surprised to see that a herd of cattle had prior possession of it. Scrub and live oak dotted the landscape, as well as the ever-present baccaris. Right before them was a water trough.

Suddenly the hounds gave voice. Rosemary shivered. Heavens, she told herself, if the hunt was this exciting just to watch, what would happen if she ever had a chance to ride in one? She'd probably fall off and disgrace herself—or faint dead away.

She feasted her eyes on the color before her, the black and tan and white of hounds, the scarlet coats against black and bay horses, the grays and chestnuts in the field and, everywhere, a background of green hills and blue sky in sharp, clear winter sunshine. The sounds that reached her were harmoniously blended together— the hounds, the plaintive notes of the horn, the hoof beats of horses, the crack of a whip in the air. She'd never forget it—not a single thing!

The riders were swallowed up in the trees and it was

over! The pack milled about for a time and finally gave up.

Suddenly a lone hound appeared in front of them, tired and hot, too thirsty to care about discipline. She had searched out the water trough and blissfully lowered herself in it until only her head was visible, lapping with her pink tongue as she lolled in solitude. As soon as she'd refreshed herself sufficiently, she joined the pack, cautiously skirting it and easing herself in inconspicuously amongst the others. Rosemary lost track of her and wondered, as the entire pack of hounds descended on the water, if she would feel obligated to go back in to keep up appearances.

All the hounds fell into the trough, sterns waving in the air, biting at the water, shaking themselves and frolicking. They were like a class of first-graders let out for recess, Rosemary thought. As suddenly as they had appeared, they left, trotting docilely towards home.

Mr. Sedgwick waved his hunting whip at her as he passed and called, "How did you like it, Rosemary?"

She let out her breath in a long sigh of satisfaction and answered, "Wonderful."

She was content to let Mrs. Hopkins and Bob do all the talking on the way back. She didn't want to ask questions now—it was enough just to think of what she had seen.

Half the fun of the hunt, Rosemary discovered later at brunch, was in talking about it. Brunch, which she privately thought of as more of a party, was at the Clayton home and everyone at the meet had been invited.

Mr. Sedgwick explained it all as they hacked home. "Mrs. Sedgwick and Cindy are coming, too," he said.

Then he told her everything that had taken place on the runs she hadn't been able to see. By the time they reached the barn, she felt as though she had galloped every hill and jumped every fence.

Rosemary was introduced to the Claytons and then Pete came along and steered her towards some of his friends and they all ate together on the flagstone terrace.

It was fun just listening. Everyone had an experience that was uniquely his own and everyone wanted to talk about it—even the man who'd had a spill when his horse was practically standing still.

Cindy walked slowly by and Rosemary smiled at her. Cindy said, "Hi," as though she hadn't ridden in the same car with Rosemary a little while before.

"Hi," Rosemary and Pete said together.

"Cindy," Pete continued, "when your Dad has the safest horse in the hunt in Sea, why don't you come out with us some time? Get Rosemary to give you some jumping lessons. I'll bet she'd be a good teacher."

Cindy gave Pete a long-suffering look and turned on her heel.

4. *Cindy Learns to Ride*

A month had gone by since Rosemary had watched the hunt but she still thought about it almost constantly. As she got off the school bus on a rainy Friday afternoon, she wished for the thousandth time that she had a horse of her own and belonged to the Las Parra Hunt. She wondered dismally if it would ever happen.

She hadn't seen Mr. Sedgwick since she'd ridden Sea for him that Saturday. Now that she knew him, she couldn't very well sit under an apricot tree and "spy" on him. Besides, it was muddy in the orchard and too cold. All that remained was to relive the hunt again and again in her imagination.

She could still see the horses galloping over the rolling

33

fields, jumping fences and pulling up sharply for the turns. She could see gray horses and browns and chestnuts in the clear winter sunshine of that February day. The lady who rode side-saddle, the children, the timid and the fearless paraded before her eyes. It was like a moving picture that unreeled itself for her at will. She never grew tired of it.

She could almost smell the redwood trees, the tender green grass, and the sweaty horses as they galloped past. And she could almost hear the hounds and the horn and the crack of the hunting whip.

"Mr. Sedgwick phoned today," her aunt greeted her as she walked into the kitchen. "He has to go on a business trip. He wanted to know if your uncle and I would mind if you took care of his horses for two weeks while he's gone. He offered to pay you."

"What did you say?" Rosemary asked anxiously, the hunt forgotten.

"I *knew* you'd want to and I was sure it would be all right with your Uncle Ed. You spend all your time mooning over horses—you might as well get paid for it."

Rosemary gave her surprised aunt a hug. She hadn't meant to sound sarcastic; she just didn't understand about horses.

"Mr. Sedgwick wants you to go over this afternoon— so he can show you where he keeps the feed and the rest of it," her aunt finished her message.

Rosemary changed her clothes quickly, eager to find out more about her job. Gosh! Mr. Sedgwick wouldn't have to pay her! To have *two* horses to ride and take care of for two weeks—it was the nicest thing that had

34

happened in a long time. She could hardly wait to get there. She put on jeans and a turtle-neck sweater that had once belonged to her father. Repeated washings had shrunk it down almost to her size and it was warm.

Mr. Sedgwick was taking a sack of grain out of his station wagon when she came up the driveway. She'd had to go around on the road because the orchard was too wet and she was breathless from going so fast.

"Hello, Rosemary. Did your aunt tell you I called?"

"Yes, she did. When are you leaving?"

"Sunday. As soon as I get this feed put away, I'll show you where I keep everything.

"I certainly appreciate your taking on this job for me. Neither Mrs. Sedgwick nor Cindy can take care of the horses. They could feed if I were going away overnight, but not for two weeks. It's too much of a responsibility. Then I'd still have to get someone to exercise the horses. I hope I'm not giving you too much of a job." He looked at her as though trying to decide if she were really up to it.

"It won't be too much, honest!" she said quickly, afraid he might change his mind.

"I know you like horses, but having to clean two stalls every day is a chore and riding two horses is wearing. When it isn't raining and if the paddocks aren't too muddy, you can turn them out during the day. Otherwise they're a handful to ride. Maybe you'd better longe both of them before you ride—to be on the safe side. Actually, Understudy isn't a problem when you're hacking him. He only resents too much pressure with your legs and close work."

Rosemary could feel herself smiling at Mr. Sedg-

35

wick's serious expression and couldn't help a chuckle. "Sounds like grand fun," she said at his look of surprise.

She set her alarm to ring an hour earlier so she could feed and water the horses before she left for school. The rain held off and she turned them out every morning.

On the third afternoon she had an unexpected visitor. As she was putting a saddle on Understudy, she heard footsteps in the barn. Looking around, she was surprised to see Cindy, dressed in jodhpurs and a sweater.

"Hi," said Rosemary, smiling at her.

Cindy didn't answer for a moment. Then she said, "Do-you-think-you-can-teach-me-to-ride-in-the-two-weeks-Dad-is-going-to-be-gone?" all in a rush.

"I thought you didn't like horses?" Rosemary was so surprised at Cindy's request she said the first thing that popped into her head.

"I like horses—all right." Cindy seemed to be fumbling for words. "It's just that—well—Dad isn't the easiest person to teach anyone. He expects to tell you something *once* and that then you can do it. I guess I'm dumb, but I can't remember to do so many things all at the same time."

Rosemary nodded in sympathy. "I know what you mean. No one learns from being told just once or twice. You have to be told over and over again." She was thinking of the hundreds of times she'd said, "Keep your heels down," to the pupils at the Berkeley stables where she'd worked the summer before. "Besides," she continued out loud, "everyone says it's easier to learn from an outsider than from someone in your own family.

36

"I'd love to try to help you. Sea would be a g-r-r-and horse for you to learn on." She was getting so excited, she was rolling her r's like someone fresh from Ireland, she thought. But it *was* exciting! Cindy was being friendly at last. What fun they could have together!

She'd never really had a friend. When her parents were living, they were always on the move, from race track to race track. They laid over every winter at Pleasant Valley, while she went to school, but even then it was hard to make friends. When you lived in a small house trailer and had chores like helping with horses after school, there wasn't much time for sociability.

Not that she hadn't loved every minute of it—not that she didn't wish with all her heart, every day of her life, that she was still living in that little trailer. But now she had a friend in Mr. Sedgwick—and *at last* she was going to have a girl friend.

"If we work hard, we'll give your father the surprise of his life," she promised. "Oh, it's going to be fun! That is, if your mother approves. Did you ask her?"

Cindy's level gaze was on Rosemary but no trace of a smile showed on her face. "Yes, I asked her. She'll pay you extra for your trouble."

An icy chill swept over Rosemary. Cindy didn't want friendship—she was hiring a riding teacher! Rosemary's glance went to her hands which had automatically picked up the saddle skirt and Understudy's leather girth. She buckled it, dropped the skirt, and said in a slightly muffled voice, "I'll be happy to teach you everything I can in the next two weeks.

"Your father is already paying me for taking care of his horses. I don't want anything more from your

37

mother." She gulped and blinked her eyes fast to keep the tears from spilling over before she looked back at Cindy. "Would you like your first lesson today?"

"Yes."

"Have you ridden at all?" She tried to make her voice business-like.

"A few times. Dad gave me some lessons but—" she shrugged her shoulders.

"Let's start from the beginning anyway. We can review what you already know. When we come to something new, we can go slower.

"Let's start with putting a saddle and bridle on a horse. Your father sets great store on someone who can do these things."

She explained each step as she went along, trying to put Cindy's unfriendliness out of her mind. She explained the difference between a snaffle bit, which was usually used on Sea, and the bit and bradoon with which Understudy was worked. She showed Cindy why it was important to make sure the saddle pad was smooth and why the girth should be kept loose until after the horse had been walked a few steps.

She wasn't worried that Sea would be too much horse for Cindy, no matter how much of a beginning rider she was. Rosemary had already worked both horses on a longe line. She had to admit to herself that she hadn't really done it because Mr. Sedgwick had warned her— exactly. It was a good excuse to spend more time with them.

She showed Cindy how to gauge the length of her stirrups by measuring the leather with her outstretched arm. When she was mounted, Rosemary showed her another way to test the length of her stirrups, with her feet hanging loose and the iron hitting the ankle bone.

When Cindy was sitting comfortably on the gray horse, Rosemary told her to stand in her stirrups. "Now, look down at your feet," she directed. "You'll see that your legs are straight under you and that you can barely see the tip of your boots. That's where your legs should be . . ." she searched for the right word . . . "forevermore," she finished solemnly.

"Any time you feel your legs shifting back or forward, stand up in your stirrups and get the right leg position again. You can do this at a walk as well as when your horse is standing still. Look down at your feet and sit in the saddle again *without shifting your leg position!* This will be the most important thing you'll learn. If you have a good seat, everything else will be easy.

"The next thing to learn is to keep your heels down. A good way to limber up your ankles so that you *can* keep your heels down is to practice rotating your ankles. Like this," and she illustrated. "Practice every chance you have—when you're eating, reading, studying—whenever you're sitting down. You could even practice standing up—but only one foot at a time."

This made Cindy laugh and, after a startled moment, Rosemary joined in. Maybe Cindy didn't really hate her, she thought. Maybe in the next two weeks. . . .

They circled the ring side by side. As tactfully as she knew how, Rosemary explained how the reins should be held. Remembering what Cindy had said about her father being too critical, she thought that being tactful with Cindy would be the best way to boost her confidence, not only in herself but in her teacher.

39

"Let's try a trot now," she suggested. "Squeeze with your legs." Sea, with little urging, moved forward and Rosemary brought Understudy even with him. "Keep your hands quiet. Push yourself out of the saddle with your legs, not with your hands. Now—up, down, up, down. You're doing fine. Up, down, up, down—"

They trotted for short periods only so Cindy wouldn't tire and throw herself off balance. With frequent rests and settling herself in the saddle again, Cindy began to look better and better. Rosemary told her so frequently.

Mrs. Sedgwick came down to the ring just as Rosemary decided her pupil had had enough for the first lesson.

"I didn't want to come out sooner because I was afraid I'd bother you—so I peeked from the window. You're both wonderful! Cindy's father won't believe his eyes when he comes back."

Cindy's delight showed in her face. Her eyes sparkled as she beamed and patted Sea on the neck. "Won't it be fun, Mother? We'll make his eyes pop out for sure!"

"I've been thinking," Mrs. Sedgwick went on. "Cindy's getting along so much better than I dared hope. Do you suppose—if I borrow some horses from the Randolphs—that you could continue the lessons after Mr. Sedgwick comes back? I could drive you both over there in the car.

"Rosemary, do you think Cindy would be ready for the Novice Horsemanship Class in the hunter trials on May 15th? That's a month and a half away. I thought it would be a wonderful surprise for Jonathan to see her first in a ring. Wouldn't it be fun, girls?"

Rosemary looked at Cindy and was surprised to see a

40

pleading look on her face. Rosemary couldn't help but smile at her reassuringly before she addressed her mother. "She can be ready if she's willing to work hard. It's up to her."

"Oh, I will, I will," Cindy promised fervently.

Rosemary had never seen her show so much emotion and had never liked her so much as at that moment. Learning to ride to please her father meant a great deal to her.

On Saturday, Rosemary suggested they go for a long ride on the trail, perhaps over to the Randolph place.

She worked both horses on the longe line first. "This is the best way to exercise a horse if you don't have enough time to ride or if it's too wet—or if they've been standing without being worked too long.

"Your horse is free, yet you control his actions by the line snapped to his halter. He won't get hurt on a longe line as he's apt to do if he's turned loose in a ring to exercise himself." She gave an involuntary shudder and Cindy started to look alarmed.

"What's the matter?" she asked.

"Oh, I'm sorry. I was remembering a horrible accident I saw at the stables in Berkeley where I worked. A man turned his horse loose in the ring after it had stood in a stall for almost a week. The ring was wet and slippery.

"It's all right to let a horse buck and play at the end of a longe line. You still control his speed. But loose . . ." she shuddered again and said, "Enough lecturing for the day."

Leaving the confinement of the riding ring was a treat for the horses and it seemed to Rosemary that

41

Cindy was friendlier than she'd ever been before. The crisp air, the sharp smell of trees and grass, the occasional wild flowers, and the birds singing in the meadows could work their magic spell on anyone, she guessed.

Cindy had been talking about her father and went on and on. Rosemary was only half-listening; mostly she was enjoying her surroundings until a change in Cindy's voice caught her attention. "Your father isn't living, is he, Rosemary?"

"No."

"Did he teach you to ride? I think Dad said one time you started riding when you were a year old. Wow! I wish Dad had started with me then. He might not have been so impatient."

"My father had more time to spend with me because his job was always with horses. It was easy. I learned everything without really knowing that I was learning. It was like a baby starting to walk."

There was a short silence and then Cindy said, "I'm sorry your parents aren't living, Rosemary. It must be awfully ha—" She didn't finish the sentence.

"Thank you," Rosemary said quietly. "It is hard but I'm getting used to it." Not really, she thought to herself. She'd never get used to it. Never!

It was a relief to get to the Randolph place. She said, "We're going to play 'follow-the-leader.' " She explained, "I won't do anything you can't do. Stay right behind me and put your horse into whatever gait my horse goes in."

She started off at a trot, following the fence line in the field, changing directions diagonally and then cantering up a small hill and down the other side. She stopped when she reached the panel into the next field.

"Ohhhh! That was fun," said a slightly out-of-breath Cindy.

"I'm going to take down the top bar so we can go through the fence," Rosemary told her. "It'll be even more fun on the other side."

She stepped over the bar, Understudy chose to jump it. Sea followed, lifting each leg gingerly over the eighteen-inch obstacle.

"Shorten your stirrups one notch, Cindy," Rosemary said as she replaced the top bar in the fence. "We're going to pretend we're hunting." Cindy gave a gasp. "Don't worry, I mean without the jumps. Take a shorter rein, lean slightly forward in your saddle and grip with your knees.

"When I raise my hand like this," and she illustrated, "that means we're going to slow down. Ready?"

At Cindy's nod, Rosemary remounted and took up a canter. Every once in a while she turned around to look at Cindy, and smile at her encouragingly. She was doing fine. She was probably a little frightened, judging by the set look on her face, but she'd get over it.

They cantered single file to the creek. Rosemary raised her arm to signal a change in pace and headed Understudy towards the rushing water.

"There's nothing to this but you might get splashed a little," she announced. "Sit up straight going downhill and forward again when you're going up the bank on the other side."

She held Understudy down to a walk. At the top of

the bank she gave Cindy a moment to readjust herself in the saddle and then they cantered again.

Cindy was now much more relaxed and looked pleased as punch. Rosemary increased Understudy's gait and soon both horses were galloping. The wind stung her face and she could feel her braids flying behind her.

Sea, perfect gentleman that he was, didn't try to make a race of it. She tightened her fingers on Understudy's reins and brought him back until the two horses were galloping side by side.

"I never knew horses could be so much fun!" Cindy shouted breathlessly.

Rosemary smiled. A moment later she lifted her arm and called, "Hoooo-oh!" and together they brought their mounts down to a walk.

"I don't much care if I ride in a show or not," Cindy said a few moments later, still panting from the last gallop. "What I want is to be able to ride with Dad— and keep up with him. If I could do that—" she looked a little self-conscious at her outburst and didn't finish.

"You kept up with me today, didn't you? You'll get your wish," Rosemary promised.

Suddenly she thought she knew why Cindy disliked her. Cindy didn't want to share her father with Rosemary! Supposing she stopped giving her lessons? OH! She *couldn't* do that! It would be mean and spiteful. Besides, she loved helping Cindy, no matter what the result might be.

It was wonderful to be needed. It was wonderful to have Mr. Sedgwick need her to take care of his horses, to have Cindy need her to learn to ride. But when she had taught her all she could—Rosemary would lose everything again—just as she had in the past.

If only there was someone who would need her for always! If she only had a family—or a horse. Uncle Ed and his wife and Bruce and Joe didn't need her. They acted as though she weren't there most of the time. And sometimes she felt as though she was in their way.

Lost in her doleful thoughts, she was brought back to the present by Cindy's surprised voice, "Hey! It's starting to rain. We'll get all wet!"

5. Fallow Field

Mr. Sedgwick declared his horses had never looked better when he returned from his trip. They had shed out their winter coats almost entirely and were sleek and well-groomed.

They ought to look good, Cindy told Rosemary privately, they'd had two people slaving over them for two weeks. Unfortunately, Cindy added, she couldn't take any of the credit.

Rosemary had been invited for dinner the day after Mr. Sedgwick came home. This was the first time she'd ever been asked to go anywhere by herself, she realized. She wished she had something new and pretty to wear.

Her best dress was a corduroy jumper, saved for

church on Sunday. She was awfully tired of it but she had no choice. She steamed it in the bathroom, with the hot water tap running, hoping to raise the nap.

Maybe if she did something different to her hair, she thought, she'd look more dressed-up. She brushed it until it shone. Free from its usual braids, it curled up until it touched her shoulders. She decided to let it hang free, the top caught by a barrette of silver with turquoise stones. Her father had bought it for her in a shop on Olvera Street, the Mexican quarter in Los Angeles.

"Your hair looks lovely," Mrs. Sedgwick said, as she took Rosemary's old school coat.

"You don't know how lucky you are to have naturally curly hair," Cindy volunteered.

"Wait'll the boys see you," Mr. Sedgwick teased. "They'll beat a path to your door."

"Go along with you," Rosemary protested, startled at her own words once they were out. She had sounded exactly like her father.

As they sat in the candle-lit dining room, Mr. Sedgwick talked about his trip. He'd seen horses and horse people, of course. Rosemary was sure there would always be time for that and he'd always find them, no matter where he went.

"I stopped at Knocknagree. I've heard so much about it lately. I wanted to see what it was like. If you had the slightest interest in riding, Cindy, I'd send you there next summer."

The girls looked interested. Mrs. Sedgwick asked, "What is it, dear? It seems to me I've heard something about it myself."

"It's a riding school—a tremendous thing. And, in addition, there's a boarding and training stable.

"The school is like nothing I've ever seen before in California. The sessions are a month long and pupils live right at the school. Riding and jumping are only a part of what they learn. They're taught to take care of their own horses, feed, clean stalls, tack, everything. It's wonderful discipline and a concentrated education in everything pertaining to a horse. I wish . . ." his voice faded away without finishing the sentence.

Rosemary didn't dare look up. She felt as if she were going to explode. If he only knew it—Cindy could do a pretty fair job right this minute of taking care of a horse!

Mr. Sedgwick asked a question about his own horses and Rosemary answered, choosing her words carefully so that nothing about Cindy would slip out. When she could trust herself to glance around the table, she saw that Cindy's eyes were merry. Even Mrs. Sedgwick looked pleased about something.

The day after the dinner party it rained and rained for almost a week. With fresh signs of spring appearing overnight, Rosemary enjoyed the showers. The smell of the wet earth in April was truly one of the wonders of the world, she thought. It was so fresh and clean.

It seemed to her that the showers, and the very air she breathed, were stirring all living things, telling the trees to clothe themselves more elaborately, coaxing the grass to grow taller, the birds to rejoice in new life.

Spring rains were beautiful, Rosemary thought, as she walked bareheaded from the school bus stop. It was dark winter storms she didn't like. She always worried about horses then. Not any particular horse—but all horses. Even when she'd been a little girl, if she awakened during the night to hear the rain beating down on the roof, she'd think of all the horses in pastures and on far-away ranges.

Her father always told her they got along well enough. They could find trees and gullies for protection from the wind and rain. She knew they grew long winter coats for warmth. But she'd always wished she could bring them all into warm, comfortable barns, with clean straw beds and hot bran mashes waiting for them.

Towards the end of the week, when the rain let up, Mrs. Sedgwick phoned that she'd arranged for the use of two of the Randolph horses until after the show. She and Cindy would drive by to pick her up after school if Rosemary didn't think it was too wet.

"We can find some place to ride that isn't too sloshy," Rosemary said.

The two horses were already saddled and bridled when they arrived. The man who took care of the Randolph horses said his name was Ben. He must have been lonesome for company. He talked so much, Rosemary thought they'd never get away from him long enough for the lesson.

Cindy's horse, a big chestnut thoroughbred, belonged to the Randolph girl, away at college. According to Ben, she'd won many blue ribbons in horsemanship classes on Champ, his name for the horse.

Rosemary's mount was a bay mare, a retired open jumper affectionately called Mommie. Her gaits, as Rosemary had already suspected from looking at her legs with their straight pasterns, were stiff and choppy.

49

. The two girls worked on an oval track in front of the barn. The drainage must be perfect, Rosemary thought, the footing was so good. She wondered why she hadn't noticed the barns and track when she'd come there before. They were probably hidden from the outside course by the house and trees.

Since Cindy couldn't use Sea in the equitation class and still keep her new riding skill a secret from her father, she had to have another horse. It didn't take Rosemary long to decide that Champ was going to be a good substitute. He was wise in experience, willing and patient, and Cindy got along well on him.

The days went by all too fast. The sun shone and everywhere gardens burst into bloom. Even the back porch next to Rosemary's room had its own climbing rose covered with coral buds.

Her loneliness, Cindy's obvious dislike of her, were almost forgotten in her enjoyment of a world made bright by growing things, the almost overwhelming fragrance around her, and the dazzling sunshine. Anything was possible in the springtime, Rosemary decided.

She encouraged Cindy to do a lot of trotting without stirrups. Cindy progressed to posting on the proper diagonal and changing diagonals on figure eights. Then Rosemary had her making small circles and reversing direction at a sitting trot.

Watching Cindy put her horse into a canter, Rosemary decided she'd better watch her own equitation seat. Cindy learned by watching and was beginning to ride exactly like her.

She could understand that easily enough. She had learned from her father, who had had an easy, relaxed position in the saddle. She'd been told many times she rode just like him. Her father's seat on a horse had been beautiful, she thought, but it wasn't exactly an equitation seat.

One day she suggested Cindy and she change horses. When Cindy first started out on Mommie, she looked bewildered, then frightened, and finally angry as she progressed from the mare's jerky trot to her short, choppy canter.

"Ho-oh!" Rosemary said quickly, ashamed of having been amused at Cindy's discomfort. "I should have warned you about her. There are lots of horses as rough as she is. After you've ridden longer, you won't have so much trouble. We can change back if you want."

"Thanks," said Cindy. "I'm glad I don't have to ride *her* in the equitation class. I'd probably get bounced off."

Mr. Sedgwick was true to his word about making up a team for the hunter trials. He phoned Rosemary and asked if she would like to jump with him and Pete on Saturday at the Fallow Field grounds.

"I hope you didn't mind getting up so early on a Saturday morning," he said as they started out on the horses, "but later on in the day the place is like a three-ring circus. Everyone is schooling and going every which way.

"I think you'll like the course at Fallow Field even better than the one at the Randolphs'," he continued.

Mr. Sedgewick's remark didn't begin to prepare her for what she finally saw. There were acres and acres of rolling hills. The landscape was dotted with the most picturesque jumps to be seen outside of books and magazines. And they had already passed a beautiful old barn, rows of paddocks, and an impressive riding ring, rich with brown tanbark.

Pete was already on the grounds. It turned out he lived almost next door. Pete and Mr. Sedgwick both seemed to enjoy her exclamations over everything new she saw.

"We'll show you the inside of the barn before we leave," Mr. Sedgwick promised. "You'll like that, too."

"But who does it all belong to?" Rosemary asked in awe, still unable to believe such a story-book place could exist outside of someone's imagination.

"Mr. Medford owns it," Mr. Sedgwick explained. "He keeps the kennels and hounds for us and some of the hunt members' horses. Then he has a few horses for guests to ride, some of his own, and some of his children's horses. You'll see him at the show—the girls and his son are riding. I don't know what we'd do without him as far as the hunt is concerned."

"Is there a house here, too?" Rosemary asked. Without waiting for an answer, she said—almost to herself— "Oh, I wish I could live here. I'd never want to leave!"

"Yes, there's a house. No one lives in it though. The stable manager, who is also our huntsman, is a bachelor so he can't be bothered. He has an apartment at one end of the barn. He's the only one who lives on the grounds."

"Guess what, Rosemary?" Pete said. "There's a *real* Irish bank on the course."

Rosemary laughed. "Are you sure it's *real*? What do you have on the other side? My Daddy always said it wasn't a true Irish bank without something *live* on the other side!"

Mr. Sedgwick threw back his head and roared. "I guess that'll hold you, Pete. I can just see the faces of the exhibitors if we provide a mother pig and her babies foraging under our Irish bank. I think I'll suggest it. We need an authentic touch like that.

"Well—we'd better decide who's to go first in our team. I think your mare should set the pace, Pete. Sister Sue is more or less the lightweight of the three. Understudy is too green to lead and Sea will look better in the middle because of his color. What do you think?"

"Won't Understudy pull a lot if he has to stay behind two other horses?" Pete asked.

"Let's give it a try and see if he settles down. Your mare has enough speed—she'll keep things from getting too dull for him."

Pete nodded in agreement.

Mr. Sedgwick was still discussing the way the course should be ridden. "Rosemary, we gallop and jump single file until Pete gives us a signal to move up even with him. Then we'll finish three abreast. Are you ready?"

"It's as good a time as any," she said happily. What fun this was going to be, she thought! For a change, someone else was deciding what was best and assuming all the responsibility. She hadn't realized how tense she'd felt these last few weeks with the obligation of the two horses and a beginning rider.

If the judge they would have the next day liked a fast pace, she thought, Sister Sue would be hard to beat. She jumped boldly and never had to bother to shorten stride before a jump. She was so clever she could get herself out of any situation without appearing to have been in one.

Sea, steady and stout-hearted, would always keep up. Understudy behaved because his master wasn't going to stand for any nonsense.

Her face tingling, the wind whipping tears from her eyes, her braids streaming, Rosemary hadn't a care in the world! This wasn't exactly hunting, she told herself, but it was a pretty good substitute. She hoped Mr. Sedgwick would want to school one more time.

"We veer off to the left after the worm fence," Pete shouted. He jumped it, slowed down, and said, "Come up alongside."

As soon as Rosemary went over the jump, she squeezed with her legs to increase Sea's speed and drew abreast of Pete. In a moment Mr. Sedgwick was on the other side of her.

"We have three jumps to do together, Rosemary," Mr. Sedgwick said. "After the first one, we'll make a gradual turn to the right."

She knew great skill would be required for all three of them to gallop a couple of hundred yards with a turn and three jumps and go well together. She hoped she wouldn't spoil it for the other two. Suddenly it seemed as important now as though they were being scored by a judge.

Stride for stride the horses approached the first of the three jumps, post and rails three panels wide. Understudy was being checked. Sister Sue galloped with her customary confidence; valiant Sea was not to be left behind.

It was just like flying, she thought, for all three of them to take off at the same time, soar over the jump, and land as one. Three horses moved out at the same speed.

"Perfect!" Mr. Sedgwick was so pleased he was waving his arm. "Remember how you did so we can do it again." He was starting to slow down. Rosemary brought Sea back the slightest bit and they rounded their turn smoothly.

"Ready for the count-down everybody," Pete said, "five—four—three—two—one—JUMP!" and they were over the next one.

Pete couldn't be serious about anything, Rosemary thought. But she knew better than to think he achieved such faultless performances on Sister Sue casually. He knew the way the mare liked to jump and gave her every help she needed. His hands were always light on her mouth and he was never behind.

They all three sailed over the last jump and eased up on their horses together.

"Now we make a circle at the finish," Mr. Sedgwick directed.

They pivoted around Understudy and then walked towards the stables, three sets of reins slack. Rosemary took a good look at Sister Sue. She was reddish-brown, a little lighter in color than Understudy.

She wondered again for the thousandth time which was her favorite color—brown or gray. She thought of all the beautiful brown horses she'd seen on the track. Her father had owned a seal-brown, two-year-old stallion once and she remembered a glimpse she'd had years before of a brood mare. She and her father had

55

gone to see some yearlings at a breeding farm in Pleasant Valley. The brown brood mare had been alone in a paddock under an old oak tree. Rosemary couldn't remember whether the sun shining through the tree dappled the mare's side and flank or whether it had been the mare's own dapples she'd seen. Whichever it was—it could have been yesterday—she remembered so well. And the memory of the mare's beauty still had the power to dazzle her. She could even remember her name—Transmutation! Rosemary sighed.

Silver Sea, under her, with a coat that was snow white, except for the freckles of black and gray sprinkled on his neck and flanks, was beautiful. She guessed she thought most horses were beautiful in one way or another.

Sister Sue, though, came closest to her ideal, but she belonged to Pete. Someday—there would be a horse meant for her! Perhaps it wasn't even born yet—she knew she hadn't seen it—but there had to be one—sometime!

"Rosemary, would you like to ride in an equitation class at the hunter trials?" Mr. Sedgwick asked. "They have them for all age groups, novice and open. You could use Sea."

She almost said, I know there are, before she checked herself. Instead, she thought a moment and then said, "Thanks ever so much but I don't think I should ride in an equitation class—not if I'm going to go in teams with you. It doesn't seem fair to ride with children *and* grown-ups, too, and I'd rather go in teams."

"That's certainly sporting of you," Mr. Sedgwick said, "I know how you feel."

56

"Well, if you don't want to go in an equitation class, how about riding Sister Sue in Ladies' Hunters? I've always thought I'd like to watch her go in a ladies' class some time," Pete said.

"I'd love to—if you're sure you think I can handle her all right."

"I wouldn't ask if I didn't think you could do it. How about meeting me here tomorrow and trying her out?"

"All right. What time?"

"About two o'clock. Can you make it then?" At her nod, he said, "Let's show her the stables, Jonathan."

Rosemary had the strangest feeling on entering the stables—as though she'd been there before. Everything seemed familiar. It was almost like coming home, but she couldn't remember ever having seen a barn quite like it. The stalls opened onto an inner courtyard. On the outside there was an over-hang all the way around the quadrangle of the white clapboard barn.

"How wonderful," she exclaimed. "When it rains, you can exercise horses here. You could even pony one or two if you were in a hurry." She could almost see herself on a horse, leading another one.

"Yes, you could," Mr. Sedgwick agreed. "I hadn't thought of that." He was looking at her thoughtfully but Rosemary was so excited about the strange feeling that possessed her, she didn't wonder about it until later.

She wanted to see all the horses and ran ahead of Mr. Sedgwick and Pete, peering into every stall, patting a gray and then a bay nose and rubbing the star on a chestnut forehead.

6. *"And What Do You Think You're Doing?"*

Rosemary was leaving the house to keep her date with Pete the next day when she was called to the phone.

"It's me, Cindy," she heard, before she'd finished saying "Hello."

"Dad's going to be gone all afternoon and I was thinking—wouldn't it be fun for a change to ride Champ and Mommie over to Fallow Field? Don't you think it would be good experience for me?"

"Well—yes," Rosemary said hesitantly. An anxious glance at the clock told her she barely had time to get to the hunter trial grounds by two o'clock. "But

I'm supposed to be there in twenty minutes to ride Pete's mare over the outside course. . . ." her voice faded as she considered. "Cindy, maybe I could phone Pete and tell him I'll be a little late and go with you. . . ." Before she had a chance to finish her sentence, Cindy said, "Oh—never mind!" and hung up.

"Gosh!" Rosemary said aloud as she put the receiver back. "*Now,* what did I say wrong?" She'd only said that she had to meet Pete, she thought, and she'd better hurry or she'd be late.

Pedalling her bike as fast as she could, she thought about Cindy. This was the first time Cindy had ever called her, and Rosemary'd had to turn her down! Cindy just didn't give her enough time to think of anything. Darn!

Rosemary arrived at Fallow Field to see Pete standing in front of the stables, talking to two girls. Rosemary hesitated and then stopped her bike before she reached them.

"Hi, Rosie," Pete called. "Have you met Debbie and Anne Medford yet? They're going to be your competition in the Ladies' Hunter Class."

"So you're the lucky one who gets to ride Sister Sue," said a dark-haired girl, in the most beautiful breeches and boots Rosemary had ever seen. And she was about the most beautiful girl she'd ever seen, too, Rosemary decided.

"Pete always said the mare was too complicated for a *girl.* You must be quite a rider." It was the younger of the two talking, very nearly as pretty as her sister and with the same dark hair and blue eyes.

"Hey—do you know that Rosemary almost looks like

59

she could be related to you two? Maybe it's because you all have the map of Ireland on your faces." Pete had to duck as both sisters started pounding on him.

"We could at that, couldn't we, Anne?" Debbie asked.

"Never," Rosemary said emphatically. "You girls are much too pretty."

"Well, thank you."

"Thanks." The sisters spoke almost together.

"If the local admiration society will pardon an interruption—let's get started," Pete said. "I promised my family I'd be home by five o'clock.

"Why don't we all walk down and watch Rosie jump? Here—you might as well get on the mare now. I'll give you a leg up."

Rosemary was in the saddle before she had a chance to protest. She shortened her stirrups and wished fervently that Pete hadn't suggested the girls watch her. They were awfully nice but they made her self-conscious.

Picking up the laced snaffle rein, she looked towards Sister Sue's small ears and suddenly didn't care whether the girls watched or not. Pete was letting her ride his mare. She didn't know why he was being so kind, but she was going to do her best to justify his confidence. Besides—Sister Sue was one of the most beautiful horses she'd ever sat on and she would enjoy every minute of her ride.

"Do you know how the course goes?" she asked.

"I do—sort of vaguely," Debbie answered. "I think they plan to leave out some of the more trappy jumps. You're safe enough if you start over there," pointing,

60

"and go around that way, down the hill, through the trees and finish over there."

"Any instructions?" Rosemary asked, turning to Pete.

"I don't need to give you any," he said complacently. "You know how the mare goes—and I know how you go."

Rosemary shook her head in mock despair and Anne said, "He's a big help, isn't he?"

"I think I'll work her a little first to get used to her," Rosemary decided.

"Help yourself," said Pete. "And good luck, Rosie."

She walked the mare away from the group and instantly forgot them. Describing a large circle around the first jump, she put Sister Sue into a trot. Somehow, she just knew she'd have a trot so smooth she'd barely need to rise out of the saddle on a post. She brought the mare down to a halt, closed the fingers of her right hand on the rein, and moved her right leg behind the mare's girth. Sister Sue responded with a canter on the left lead, as smooth as a canoe gliding through water.

Rosemary reversed direction. At the precise moment the mare returned to the circle, Rosemary shifted her weight back and to the left, repeated the closing of her fingers, this time with her left hand, and used her left leg behind the girth. Sister Sue changed leads effortlessly. After cantering her twice around the circle, Rosemary brought her down to a walk and turned towards the first jump.

"Now I see why Pete is letting you show Sister Sue," Debbie called to Rosemary.

"And I might not bother going in the class at all," Anne sighed.

Only Pete had nothing to say. He just stood there with a big grin on his face.

"I'd better get started before the course gets too crowded," Rosemary said, embarrassed by the extravagant compliments. A number of horses and riders had appeared while she was working the mare and more were to be seen coming from the barn.

She circled and headed for the post and rail. "Remember how light Pete's hands always are," she warned herself, and guided the mare as though she were holding silken threads instead of reins.

Sister Sue was being as wary of Rosemary as she was of the mare. She went over the first jump more cautiously than Rosemary had ever seen her go. As they galloped to the second fence, the mare's ears moved back and forth rapidly. Suddenly they stayed forward and she jumped—came down—and for the first time Rosemary felt her tremendous power as they galloped on towards the next fence.

Now she was going the way she went for Pete—with faultless coordination, bold and true, and swift as the wind.

Afterwards, Rosemary could barely remember which jumps she'd gone over. She felt as though she'd been to another world and it was strange having to come back to earth.

Pete must have understood even though she was too dazed to say anything. He looked very knowing and only said he was glad he'd waited to find a rider.

He introduced her to the group who had stopped to watch her jump. There were so many people, she couldn't keep their names straight.

Riding her bike home, she thought about them. She remembered Mr. Medford because he was Debbie and Anne's father and because he owned the beautiful course she'd ridden over.

He was tall, gray-haired, and heavy and didn't ride although he seemed to know a great deal about horses. And then he had said the strangest thing. When they were introduced, he'd said, "So you're the young lady with the interesting background Jonathan's been telling me about."

The others had been all ages and sizes and apparently members of the hunt. They were friendly and interested and acted as though they really wanted to see her do well in the show. It gave her a pleasant glow to think how nice they'd been. Mostly, though, she thought about the ride she'd had on Sister Sue.

As the date of the hunter trials drew closer, everything became more and more hectic. Rosemary inventoried her meager stock of riding clothes for the Sedgwicks and they volunteered to borrow a black riding coat and hunting cap for her.

Pete was going to get a hunting whip and sandwich case from his mother for her appointments in the Ladies' Class and Teams. The Sedgwicks had extra white stocks and Rosemary bought a pair of yellow string gloves with her small savings.

She sent her only jodhpurs to the cleaners, polished her worn jodhpur shoes until she could almost see her face in them, and starched the collar and cuffs of a white shirt Bruce had outgrown.

Now when she gave Cindy a lesson, she had to wear jeans and canvas sneakers. Cindy found excuses to phone even though she saw Rosemary at school and had riding lessons almost every day. Rosemary wasn't too sure so many lessons were necessary, but if she wasn't there to watch Cindy every minute, she seemed to lose confidence.

Privately Rosemary thought Cindy would be better off if she hacked her horse alone on the trail. Then she could apply some of the things she learned, as she thought of them, and in time good horsemanship would become an unconscious habit.

Mrs. Sedgwick was the busiest of all. In addition to finding clothes for Rosemary and getting Cindy to the show without her father seeing her, she had other duties. She was on the Refreshment Committee and had to prepare and take to the show grounds dozens and dozens of sandwiches. Rosemary and Cindy helped her shop and spent the day before the show making fillings and wrapping sandwiches in neat squares of wax paper.

The Randolphs' stableman would bring Champ to the show by trailer. Mr. Sedgwick planned to haul his two horses also and he and Rosemary would braid their manes and tails at home.

The horsemanship classes, ladies' hunters, and green hunters, in which Mr. Sedgwick was showing Understudy, were to be held in the morning.

The highly prized Master's Cup and Field Master's Plate were to be held in the afternoon. Mr. Sedgwick had donated the perpetual trophy for this class. Pete was trying for that and Mr. Sedgwick was competing for the Master's Cup which Sea had won two years before. Hunt Teams was the last class of the day.

Mr. Sedgwick was methodical and efficient and he

and Rosemary pulled out of the driveway early the morning of the show. She was lucky, Rosemary decided, that he had promised to help some of the committee people on last-minute details at the show grounds. They would get there early enough so she could help Cindy get ready for her class. Besides, it would be more fun. She'd have that much more time to see everything!

Mr. Sedgwick even had a stable boy waiting for him, who was going to watch the horses.

"But I could do it," Rosemary protested.

"Not all day—you wouldn't have a chance to see the show. It's all arranged—so you wander around and enjoy yourself. Pete will find you pretty soon and Mrs. Sedgwick and Cindy will be here after a while." He was already being pressed into service to decide if a field judge was necessary for the farthest jumps.

Sea and Understudy were contentedly munching hay in the trailer. Rosemary wandered around light-heartedly, watching horses being unloaded, calling back a "Good morning" to the friendly people who smiled and greeted her as she passed.

It wasn't just the early morning sunshine that made her feel as though something inside of her were melting. This new inner warmth came from the people she passed. They made her feel as though she were one of them, as though she belonged. Not for a long time had she felt so at home.

She hummed happily as she side-stepped a cranky mare that looked as though she might let fly with a hind leg.

"Say—do you know how to tie one of these darn things?"

She turned to see a small boy on a rangy chestnut horse right beside her. He had a worried expression on his face as he fumbled with a bulging knot of white piqué stock with one hand and held a fistful of tangled reins with the other.

"I think so. You'll have to get off your horse first though."

"It was all right when I started out and now it's poking out funny," he said with disgust.

As he slid off his horse, Rosemary held the reins and then drew them over the horse's head.

"I'll hold the reins and you can hold this," she said, undoing the gold safety pin and handing it to him. "Get your chin up," she directed. "Now—let's see. What was it my Daddy used to say? Left over right—or was it right over left?"

She adjusted the stock to her liking and then pinned it securely. "What class are you going in?"

"Novice—ten and under," he said indistinctly, his chin high in the air so he wouldn't get stuck with the pin.

"I'm finished now—you can get your head down. You don't sound like you're very happy about riding in the show."

"I'm not—very much." He lowered his head and she was looking into a pair of blue eyes so like her own she might have been looking in a mirror. She wondered if her eyes ever looked as worried as his did.

"Don't you like to ride?" she asked.

"Well—sometimes—but not today. I forgot my glasses again—and I'm not a very good rider."

"Really? You know—looking at you I'd say you *were*

66

a good rider. You look like you have good hands on a horse. And that's about the most important thing."

He looked down at his hands in surprise, blinking his eyes, and tentatively wiggled a couple of fingers.

"Do you want a leg up?" Rosemary asked.

"Yes, please."

When he was in the saddle, she automatically shifted his foot in the stirrup so the iron was on the ball of his foot.

"Do you always ride with such a long stirrup or did you put this one down so you could get on easier?"

"No, I usually get on by the fence, or someone helps me."

She walked around the horse to the other side and said, "This stirrup over here is about two holes shorter than the other one. Let's see which way is the most comfortable for you."

She shortened the near stirrup, tested the length against his ankle, told him to sit up straight, and then went to the front of the horse to see if both stirrups were even. "Does that feel comfortable?" she asked.

"I think so," he said, standing in his stirrups and sitting down a few times to test them.

"Now you'll be able to keep your heels down better," she said as he fumbled trying to pick up his reins.

"Did you ever do it this way?" she asked, picking up the double reins and sliding them through her fingers with a single motion.

They were both so intent on his getting the top rein between the proper fingers, she didn't turn around when she felt someone stopping beside her.

"And what do you think you're doing?" a voice asked, the tone heavy with sarcasm.

Rosemary dropped the reins and stepped back—as though she'd been caught doing something wrong.

A stocky red-haired man, with jodhpurs skin-tight from the knee down and a billowing peg from the knee up, scowled at her. His small eyes seemed to shoot sparks from under the visor of a checked cap, a cigarette dangled from the corner of his mouth.

"She was just showing me how to hold the reins, Red."

"And how many hundreds of times have I shown you how to hold the reins?" the man asked, mimicking the way the little boy talked.

Rosemary could feel herself flushing with embarrassment. Why was he so angry? They hadn't done anything wrong.

"Well—she showed me a way I can understand." The little boy sounded defiant.

The man he called Red looked at him a moment, glared at Rosemary, and, with a "Hummmh!" that showed his contempt for them both, turned and left.

"I hope I didn't get you into any trouble," she said when the man was out of sight. "Who is he?"

"He's supposed to be teaching me to ride," the boy said with a sigh of resignation.

Rosemary looked at his sad little face with the worried blue eyes and suddenly folded her arms pompously, blew her cheeks out as she leaned back and cocked her head. "And what do you think you're doing?" she said, tapping her foot and trying to make her voice even more ferocious than the man's had been.

68

The little boy's eyes widened and his mouth fell open. After a startled moment, a small laugh escaped. "I'm just sitting on my horse," he said grinning. "Say," he continued, peering down at her, "what's your name?"

"Rosemary. What's yours?"

"Billy."

"Hi, Billy. That reminds me, I want to look at my time sheet." She took a folded paper out of her pocket and said, "You're in the second class, aren't you?"

"I don't know. Am I?"

"Yes, you are. And I have a pupil going in the novice class right after yours—the 10 to 14 years." She thought a moment. "I think I'd better get back to the horses now, Billy. But I'll see you at the back gate before your class. Then I can check on your stock. All right?"

He nodded as he looked at her. "Don't forget," he called as she walked away.

The smile faded from her face. She'd been so happy just a few minutes before, and then that awful Red had to come along. She knew trainers didn't like interference but she really hadn't meant to meddle. She'd only tried to help Billy feel more comfortable in the saddle. And he *hadn't* known how to pick up the reins too well—nor hold them.

She thought of Cindy, who didn't want her for a friend—and now this man, whose dislike of her showed so plainly. She shook her head, as though by that action she would be rid of him.

7. *Equitation Class*

Cindy came to meet Rosemary as she was walking slowly back towards the trailer area. After that, it was easier not to think about Red. She could concentrate on her.

Ben had parked the Randolph trailer as far away from Mr. Sedgwick's as he could and posted himself as look-out. Mrs. Sedgwick was moving things around in the back of her station wagon nearby.

"You look wonderful," Rosemary said to Cindy, noticing her new tweed riding coat for the first time, fawn-colored jodhpurs, and velvet hunting cap.

"Thanks," Cindy said in a slightly shaky voice. Her

eyes weren't sparkling now as they usually did. There was a sort of glaze over them, Rosemary saw.

They could hear the loudspeaker, calling the first class. Ben started to bridle and saddle Champ.

"Is it time to go *already?*" Cindy asked.

Mrs. Sedgwick stopped what she was doing and looked up quickly.

"It's a little early," Rosemary answered, "but why don't you take Champ down beyond the paddocks? Your father won't go there and it will be more relaxing than standing around here thinking about your class.

"I'll come and get you when it's time," she called to Cindy's receding back.

"That reminds me, Rosemary," Mrs. Sedgwick said, "I have a black coat for you to wear and—something else."

She took a box from the station wagon. "This is a present for you from Cindy and me," she said, holding out the square box. "It doesn't begin to show our appreciation. You've been so patient with Cindy and given up so much of your free time."

"I haven't anything else to do with my free time," Rosemary said as she opened the box, "and I . . ." Her voice faded as she took out a black hunting cap with a famous English maker's name imprinted on the lining.

"Oooh! Thank you!" In one motion the cap was on her head, covering her curly black hair except for the ends of two braids which rested on her shoulders. "It just fits. Now I really feel as if I'm going to be in a show!"

"I'm glad you like it, dear," Mrs. Sedgwick said.

Rosemary tried on the borrowed black coat and Mrs. Sedgwick said it looked fine. Then she explained her plan to get Mr. Sedgwick into the grandstand for Cindy's class. Some friends named Tupper had a daughter riding in Cindy's class. The Tuppers, who were in on the surprise, were supposedly in need of advice on their daughter's horsemanship and whether or not she'd outgrown her horse. Mr. Sedgwick had promised to sit in their box and advise them after he watched her ride.

"I'll keep him distracted until the class gets underway," Mrs. Sedgwick finished, "and let him spot Cindy for himself.

"I guess I'd better leave now—I promised to help sell coffee for a while. You won't need my help with Cindy, will you?" she said, not waiting for an answer but starting to walk away, a harassed look on her face.

Oh, dear! thought Rosemary. If she looks that way when Mr. Sedgwick sees her, he'll know something is up. Unless she always gets nervous when she sells coffee.

Rosemary listened to the announcer's instructions over the loudspeaker and decided the first class still had a while to go. She started towards the back gate thinking maybe Billy might be there. If—that man—were with him, she'd just wave. But if he weren't, she'd check and see if Billy was all right.

The grounds had a festive air that couldn't help but excite her. Considering it was the first class and early in the morning, quite a few people were sitting in the grandstand. More spectators were coming from the stables and the parking area. The refreshment booths looked gay with bright bunting. She could see Mrs. Sedgwick handing a cup of coffee and a doughnut to the side-saddle lady.

White cardboard drums for discarded paper and

72

bottles were placed here and there. Some unknown artist had made charcoal drawings of horses on them and Rosemary had to stop and admire each one.

Finally she saw Billy, sitting on his horse, a little apart from the other children. He looked all alone and somehow strange until she decided it was because he was now wearing horn-rimmed glasses. He was still holding his reins the way she'd shown him.

Walking quietly up beside his horse, she said, "Your stock looks fine."

"Oh—hi! I was wondering if you'd get here."

"I see you have your glasses."

"Yeah. I went back to the barn and phoned home. My sister brought them."

"Have you warmed up your horse yet?" Rosemary asked.

"Well—a little, I think."

Rosemary caught sight of Red, a short distance away, talking to two men. He looked settled and relaxed, not worried about a small pupil.

"Why don't we go over there?" she suggested, pointing to a clearing where a few children were trotting and cantering their horses. "Wouldn't you like to work your horse a little before you go into the ring?"

"All right," Billy said and obediently turned his horse around.

After he had dutifully trotted and cantered his horse in a circle a few times for her, he came back and she asked, "How long have you been riding?"

"Oh—about a year or two," he said vaguely.

"Really? Uh—you did fine," she added quickly. Inwardly she was shocked to think of how weak Billy's

73

seat was on the horse—no matter what length of time he'd ridden. And he ought to wear spurs; his horse was sluggish and lazy.

"Do you really think so?" Billy asked.

"I sure do. Just remember to keep your heels down and look between your horse's ears—not down on the ground. And—most important of all—smile, Billy— as though you were enjoying yourself. With good hands and a smile, you'll always get along. I promise."

The class in the ring was lining up and soon the loud-speaker was announcing the winners. Billy joined the group waiting to go into the ring for the next class. As the children crowded together, Rosemary whispered, "Don't get too close to the horse in front of you. He might kick. Try to stay clear of the rest of the class. It's dangerous to bunch up and, besides, when you're in the ring the judge can't see you. Good luck! I'll keep my fingers crossed for you."

He flashed her a smile and turned towards the ring with squared shoulders.

She crossed her fingers and then looked around to see if anyone had noticed. She self-consciously folded her arms. There! Now if anyone looked at her, they wouldn't be able to see her hands.

Rosemary saw Red saunter up to Billy and in a loud voice say, "Go on in there and do a good job. Hear me?" and give Billy's unsuspecting horse a resounding slap on the rump that almost unseated his rider.

Who couldn't hear him? Rosemary thought indignantly. She moved to the rail so Red wouldn't notice her and focused her attention on the ring. Watching the children stream into the class on horses of all sizes, colors, and conditions, she decided there must be about thirty of them. She wondered how the judge could possibly have time to notice every one. She had a hard time keeping track of Billy, the horses bunched up so badly.

The judge allowed the entire class to work in both directions and then called about half of the riders into the center of the ring. He worked the remainder of the children on the rail and then excused all but two. These two were joined by the group that had been in the middle of the ring and more were eliminated.

Billy was in the ring until the end of the second elimination. He kept his eyes forward between his horse's ears until he got to the back gate. Then he searched for Rosemary out of the corner of his eyes and gave her a big smile which she hoped lasted all the way around the ring.

He was excused just as she decided she couldn't stay another minute. It was time to find Cindy. Rosemary was starting to walk away when he trotted his horse up beside her.

"I didn't lose my stirrups once," he said triumphantly as she stopped. "And I stayed in the class longer than Richie and Mark!"

"You looked good, too," Rosemary said. "I wanted to watch but I have to look up my pupil for the next class."

"Can I come with you?"

"Of course."

Cindy was already at the trailer with Ben.

"Hi, Billy," Cindy said.

"Hi! Is this your pupil?" he asked Rosemary.

"Yes, do you know each other?"

"Oh, yeah," Billy answered. "She knows my sisters. Say—are you riding in any classes, Rosemary?"

"I'm going in Ladies' Hunters later on this morning and Teams this afternoon."

"Well, I'll watch you. I guess I'd better take my horse back now. Red'll be looking for me."

"How'd you happen to meet *him?*" Cindy asked after Billy had left.

"Oh, he needed someone to fix his stock for him. Poor kid, he doesn't seem to have anyone to look out for him."

"Poor kid!" Cindy almost screamed. "Don't you know who he is?"

"No. Should I?"

"He's just Mr. Medford's son—that's all!"

"Really? Then he's Debbie and Anne's brother. That's funny. . . ." She shrugged and continued, "I watched the class just now and I think I know what the judge wants. It won't be anything you don't already know. Let me give you a leg up and then I'll wipe off your boots—they're all dusty."

"Oh, Rosemary, I'm scared!" Cindy turned anguished eyes toward her. "Who thought of this stupid idea, anyhow?"

"Cindy! Be quiet and listen a minute. You'll feel completely different when you get in the ring. The judge won't pay any attention to you at first. He'll be busy checking his score card and getting organized. That'll give you time to get used to everything.

"Pretend you're in the ring at home. Do as well as you've been doing every day and you'll make your father proud of you."

76

At the mention of her father, Cindy sat up straighter in the saddle. She looked down at her hands and then at Rosemary and said, "Thanks. I'll be all right now. And—thanks for everything, Rosemary. You've sure had to put up with a lot from me."

Rosemary patted the toe of Cindy's jodhpur boot and swallowed hard. She looked away and saw Mr. Sedgwick in the Tupper box. "There's your Dad, Cindy!"

"Where? Where?"

"See?" and she pointed. The Tuppers apparently had Mr. Sedgwick involved in a long explanation of something. He looked from one to the other, gesturing with his hands.

"Now's your chance," Rosemary said, and Cindy followed the other exhibitors into the ring.

As Rosemary watched the class going in, she decided there were even more riders than in Billy's class. Being older, they were more confident. The judge was giving them a good chance to show what they could do. Then he lined them up in the center of the ring and by numbers called about one-third of the group back on the rail. The rest were excused.

Rosemary's heart pounded and she held her breath as she listened to the numbers being called. Cindy was staying! Her face, under the hunting cap, looked white and set. That was her worst fault, Rosemary thought, she was too tense. Otherwise, her hands were light and quiet, her heels down, her position in the saddle fairly good and her head up, where it belonged.

Rosemary lifted her hands and pantomimed applause when Cindy came around the next time and brought a wan smile to her face. There, she was relaxing!

With a start, Rosemary realized that she'd forgotten all about sitting with the Sedgwicks. She looked over at them and saw Mr. Sedgwick grinning broadly. Cindy's mother was looking towards the ring, a proud, pleased look on her face. Rosemary didn't quite know why, but it didn't seem to be the right moment to intrude on them. Besides, now Cindy was used to seeing her at the back gate and might feel abandoned if she left.

The class was slow trotting. There were a few pretty good riders, Rosemary decided. The judge would have a difficult time making up his mind. None of them had the finished smoothness of the American Horse Show Association Medal Class competitors Rosemary had once seen. But they would have—some day. And so would Cindy if she kept riding.

Rosemary suddenly realized her forehead was damp and the palms of her hands wet. She felt the same way she used to when her father had a horse running in a race.

The most important thing was for Cindy to try her best. It would be like frosting on a cake, she thought, to have her win a ribbon, too. Any color ribbon. Well, with a little luck, and Rosemary firmly believed in luck, she might.

She could see the weaknesses of the other riders, just as she knew Cindy's weak points. Legs shifted back or forward out of position, backs stiffened, some of the riders leaned too far forward in the saddle. One boy, not trusting the feel of his horse at a canter, leaned over to see if he was on the right lead.

At last, when Rosemary was beginning to be afraid Cindy would get tired and let herself get out of position,

78

the announcer asked the class to line up. The contestants backed their horses one by one and Rosemary saw the Sedgwicks leave their seats and start for the back gate.

"Announcing winners in Class No. Three, Novice . . ." came from the loudspeaker and now Rosemary was holding her breath. "Deborah Cunningham, riding Conquering Hero, in first place. Second, Cynthia Sedgwick. . . ."

Rosemary didn't know she'd let out a whoop and was jumping up and down until the people in front of her turned around and smiled. Cindy, looking pale and glassy-eyed, was coming out of the ring just as her father reached the gate. She looked at him, a small tremulous smile showing on her face, and without a word handed him her red ribbon.

The silence was broken by Ben, coming to claim his charge. "Well, I see Champ can still earn his oats if he has to," he said in a matter-of-fact voice.

Mr. Sedgwick finally spoke. "WELL! Who says women can't keep secrets?" He scooped Cindy up as though she were a small child. "I'm so proud of you. I can't get over it!"

"Are you really, Dad?" Cindy asked.

"I sure am. Do you like horses any better now?"

"Oh, yes."

"We're going to have some high old times together, you and I. And we have a date for the very next point-to-point.

"I haven't forgotten that you did it, Rosemary. You've given me the riding partner I've always wanted." Rosemary was being enveloped in a big hug. Looking up at

79

Mr. Sedgwick, she thought she saw moisture at the corner of his eye.

"You bet Rosemary did it—every bit of it," Cindy said. Her arm went around Rosemary's shoulder and she squeezed hard.

"Good-morning, everybody!" Pete's cheery voice drawled. "I see you took my advice, Cindy. That was a good job you did with the Randolph horse."

"Were you in on this, too?" Mr. Sedgwick asked.

"No—but anyone taking a look at Rosie at the back gate, biting her nails and hopping up and down, would have known she had a hand in it."

They all moved aside as a truck, carrying jumps to be set up in the ring, honked for them to get out of the way.

"Say—do you girls want to watch the jumper class? Let's all go sit in the grandstand," Pete suggested.

Rosemary looked at Cindy questioningly. "Thanks," Cindy said, "but I think I'll go with Dad and help him get Understudy ready for the green class.

"Why don't you go with Pete, Rosemary?"

8. *Irish Hunter*

The last day of school was fun, Rosemary thought, especially now that she and Cindy were *real* friends. Ever since the hunter trials, Rosemary was included in Cindy's circle of friends, in gossip and horsy news and plans for the summer. But now Rosemary didn't have time for plans—she had her own!

As she hurried home from school for the last time until fall, she decided to put on jeans and ride her bike over to her new job. She wasn't due there until the next day, but she had already worked two week-ends and knew there was plenty to do. And now she had another reason for wanting to go.

Pedalling her bike, she thought back to the day of

the hunter trials. That was when everything had started. She wondered, for about the hundredth time, how she had lived through the excitement of that day. The hunter trials would always live in her memory as a beautiful, shimmering blur. So many wonderful things had happened, she had trouble keeping the details straight. She had to stop and think if she won a blue in the Ladies' Hunter Class with Sister Sue *before* or *after* Mr. Medford gave her a job.

She remembered that she and Pete watched the Open Jumper Class from the grandstand. Then they walked to the top of the hill to see Mr. Sedgwick get a fourth ribbon with Understudy in a class of good-looking Green Hunters.

In her mind Rosemary ticked off the highlights of that day. Where was she? Oh, yes, *then* she showed Sister Sue in the Ladies' Class. Now she had it straight!

She smiled to herself thinking of the never-to-be-forgotten ride she had on Pete's mare. It was as though Rosemary sat on four coiled springs as she waited for her number to be called. This time, Sister Sue didn't bother to size up her rider. She was ready!

Rosemary blinked her eyes, remembering how the wind had stung her cheeks as she and the mare sailed over the jumps. Sister Sue had galloped as though she wanted to get there "the fastes' with the mostes'."

Rosemary hardly remembered stepping forward for the blue ribbon. She remembered the trophy though, a beautiful silver bowl, because Pete insisted she keep it.

Then it was lunch time and they all sat together under a sprawling oak tree—the Sedgwicks, Pete, Rosemary, and little Billy. He'd offered to hand-walk Sister

Sue after her class and then stayed close by for the rest of the day.

Rosemary could still remember the lunch. It was delicious—two pieces of chicken, bread and butter, potato salad in a container, milk, and chocolate cake.

As she finished the last of her milk, she thought again that it was a perfect day. Billy grinned at her and said he wished he could have another box lunch. He was sure he could eat every bit of it except maybe the bread and butter.

Cindy asked her father if he thought she was a good enough rider now to start learning to jump. He said he sure did and he'd have her hunting "right in his pocket" in the fall. Then he looked at his wristwatch and said, "Rosemary, we have a date at the stables in about two minutes. Let's go."

"We do?" Rosemary asked in bewilderment.

"Come on." He reached for her hand and helped her up. No one said anything. Billy wasn't even looking at her. She couldn't seem to collect her wits. She'd had too much to eat, she decided. She wasn't used to so large a lunch.

They walked to the stables and neither of them said a word. Mr. Sedgwick apparently didn't want to talk about it ahead of time—whatever it was. And she couldn't tell anything by the expression on his face.

Inside, he steered her towards the office. Mr. Medford was sitting at a desk and complimented her on her ride on Sister Sue and her skill in teaching Cindy. Casually, and almost in the same breath, he asked her if she would like to work at the Fallow Field Stables through summer vacation—exercising horses and instructing children in horsemanship.

Rosemary's head whirled and before she had a chance to say more than, "Oh, yes," Billy's riding teacher, Red, sauntered by the open door.

Mr. Medford called out, "Oh, Red," and turning to her explained, "You'd better get to know our Huntsman and Stable Manager, Harry Sharpe. You'll be working with him. Red, this is Rosemary O'Connor. She's going to take some of the load off you this summer. If she wants, she can work week-ends until school lets out."

Red Sharpe had barely acknowledged the introduction. He merely grunted in her direction and said, "There's plenty to do—that's for sure."

"By the way, Red," Mr. Medford went on, "I thought Billy looked pretty good this morning in the show. You must have been bearing down on him."

And then Red's astonishing reply. "You get after kids and get after them—and finally some of it sinks in."

Get after them, indeed, Rosemary thought. He hadn't gone near Billy at the show except to hit his horse across the rump! She was so shocked at his answer she was barely aware of the sick feeling in her stomach at the thought of having to work for this man she didn't trust and was sure hated her!

How could her mind take in anything after that? Rosemary asked herself as she stood up to pedal faster. She hardly remembered riding in Teams at the hunter trials. It was a good thing she was on wise, old Silver Sea; he did it all. Thanks to the honest gray horse, Mr. Sedgwick's team placed first. She was happy for him and

Pete. For herself, she could think of nothing but her new job.

Even knowing she had to work with Red and that he was an important part of the hunt couldn't dim the excitement of the job she'd been offered. To know that she would spend every day—all day—with horses was all she could take in.

Lucky for her, too, Rosemary thought, her aunt and uncle both approved of her working. Even her cousins were impressed—probably because neither of them had found summer jobs yet.

As Rosemary parked her bike in the rack at the stables, she noticed that there were no cars around. In the stables all she could hear was the occasional stomp of a foot and the rustle of straw as one of the horses shifted position in his stall. It wasn't until she neared the tackroom that she heard voices. Don and Steve, who did all the feeding and mucking out of stalls, were cleaning saddles and bridles.

"Hi," she greeted them. "Is it always this quiet on Friday afternoon?"

"Hi," Don said, as he flipped over a saddle expertly on the sawhorse. "No, this is unusual." Don was the older of the two boys and a student at Davis College. He was working during summer vacation because he liked horses and wanted to learn everything he could about them to prepare himself for a veterinarian's job. Steve, closer to Rosemary's age, worked at the stables all year round, part-time during school and full time in summer. He wasn't as crazy about horses as Don; he worked there because he had to have a job.

"I guess this is pretty quiet," Don continued as he

buckled a girth on a saddle. "We've had a lot of cancellations. Everyone seems to be going out of town—I guess because it's the first week-end of school vacation. And Red has gone down south for a few days to look at horses," he finished with a grin on his face.

"Has he, really?" Rosemary asked and could feel the start of a smile on her own face.

"Yes—but mind no funny tricks now. That doesn't mean you're to goof off, see. Steve and I will have our eyes on you, even while we're down at the Malt Shop on a two-hour break."

Steve guffawed. He never did have much to say but enjoyed listening to Don. Rosemary smiled but her thoughts were really elsewhere. "Don, —"

"I know what you're thinking, Rosemary, and I don't approve. If you have to do something—do it while we're not around."

Rosemary was silent and finally said, "Thanks," her voice husky. "I think I'll go to the office—and check my work for tomorrow."

Outside of wishing and hoping and praying for the impossible—like having a family again—the next best thing was having a horse of her own. Oh, it was fun to ride horses, lots of horses, as she would be doing this summer. But that only whetted her appetite for one of her own! And not just *any* horse. It had to be a special one. And she'd found him! But her chance of ever owning him was fully as remote as getting a family—for he was already about half-dead!

As she sat in the office, looking with blank eyes at a hunting print on the wall, she thought back to the first time she'd seen him. Was it only two weeks ago, she asked herself in amazement? It seemed as though she had always known him.

Red had instructed a class of young children just learning to ride on her first day at work. She had helped him lead the horses out and adjust stirrups. Then she walked down to the ring and watched as the riders circled, noting the ability of the horses, the weaknesses of the children.

Red's idea of instructing was to get the class moving forward and then walk over to the fence and start a conversation with some of the spectators. He threw commands over his shoulder like "Reverse and trot," and ignored the riders for so long the horses would drag their feet in boredom and the poor children would be exhausted.

He let her take the four riders in the second class, watched her for a few minutes, and disappeared. During the noon hour, Don and Steve took the pick-up truck to town for lunch and Rosemary was alone in the stables. That was when she found her horse!

She ate her sandwich, sitting on a tackbox. After she finished, she went down the aisles, looking into each stall, getting acquainted with its occupant. She saw horses of every color, beautiful ones and a few common ones, big ones and little ones, friendly ones and cranky ones, wise ones and foolish ones. She tried to match each horse with his name and color. Then she passed empty stalls, stripped of bedding, doors open to light and air.

At the very end, next to the archway that led outside to the back of the stables, she saw a stall with the top and bottom doors closed and latched. What possessed her to look in? she wondered. She opened the top half

87

of the door and was startled to see a brown horse standing by the wall, his head low and lifeless. The near front
leg, which he was holding off the ground, was covered
from the knee down in voluminous bandages, bloody
and soiled. His neck was thin and his ribs showed, his
mane snarled with neglect, his coat stark.

"Oh, you poor, poor thing!" Rosemary exclaimed in
horror. Then she put her hand to her mouth in con-
sternation, but she needn't have worried. He paid no
attention to her. He seemed to be beyond having anything more bother him.

She shivered violently. There was a stench of dirt and
sickness and something else—an odor of death hung in
the stall.

It didn't need to be, she thought! Why wasn't the
stall immaculately clean? Why didn't he have fresh air?
His bandages were disgusting. Did they want the horse
to die?

She waited impatiently for Don and Steve to come
back so she could ask them about the poor brown horse
in the far stall.

"Don't have anything to do with him," Don said
quickly.

"If you want to get along with Red—leave him
alone," Steve echoed.

"His stall is dirty and so are his bandages. He's so
thin and weak I don't know what's holding him up!
And you say, 'Don't have anything to do with him,'
and 'leave him alone.' Is everybody crazy around here?"
Rosemary could have cried she was so confused.

Don sighed. "It's a long story. . . ." He looked as

88

though he was afraid someone would hear him. "And we don't even know too much of it.

"Mr. Medford had someone buy the horse in Ireland. When he got here, Red started to find fault with him right away. He tried jumping him and the horse fell through a jump and tore his leg wide open—clear through to the bone. So Red's taking care of him," he finished self-consciously as though even he knew how silly that sounded.

"From what I saw of him no one's taking care of him —and no one's been near him for days. Do you realize he might get a bone infection? For that matter, he might have it already!" Rosemary's voice rose higher and higher but she didn't care.

Don threw his hands out helplessly. "I admit I haven't been in his stall. Red made it plain he wanted to do it all."

"And you're going to be a vet?" Rosemary asked scornfully.

Steve looked at Don quickly but he wasn't angry at her. "I guess I deserve that, Rosemary, but when you've been here a while longer, you'll find out that when Red gives an order, he expects it to be obeyed. I only work here, I don't make the rules."

Rosemary blinked fast but couldn't keep the tears from coming.

The telephone rang then and she was too busy for a while to think about the brown horse. She waited until the lunch hour next day, when the stables were sure to be empty and quiet. Tip-toeing to the closed stall, she slowly opened the top half of the door wide enough to look in.

89

The brown horse was in the same position as he had been the day before. If anything, he looked thinner, more gaunt, his coat duller.

She gave a long, drawn-out sigh of pity. He lifted his head slightly and looked straight at her. She blinked fast but couldn't keep the tears from trickling down her cheeks.

In that slow, sorrowful look, she'd read pain and despair. He'd told her he couldn't try any longer. Tears splashed on her hands, tightly clasped in front of her as though she were saying a prayer.

9. *An Irish Friend*

As Rosemary sat in the office, she thought about the brown horse. Don had reluctantly told her his name was Dublin Jack. It didn't fit him now, but it had a beautiful sound. Dublin Jack. It would look wonderful on a name plate over his door . . . or in a horse show program . . . Dublin Jack, Rosemary O'Connor, Owner . . . or on a tombstone, she told herself bitterly.

She thought of the Irish horse, so far from the land of his birth, so neglected and friendless, with no familiar face nor voice to comfort him. "Poor little Irish," she whispered, "I have today, tomorrow and maybe the next day to take care of you. Just hang on a little longer."

Don wanted her to wait until he left before she did anything, so he wouldn't have to know about it. Well, she'd waited the whole week; she could make herself be patient a little while longer. She'd visited Irish every chance she had the week-end before and imagined he looked a little better.

She'd thought about Irish constantly the whole week. It had been hard to get to sleep at night worrying about him. She couldn't have stood it if she didn't do something. So she'd telephoned Dr. Potter, the veterinarian, whose address and phone number she'd seen on the bottles and jars of medicine and ointments in the cabinet at the stables.

At his invitation, she rode her bicycle to his office after school. He'd been so kind. Dr. Potter wasn't afraid of Red—he answered all her questions.

"I told Red that if he wasn't prepared to spend hours a day, for months, he might as well shoot the poor horse and put him out of his misery. But Red said he felt sort of responsible because he had been jumping him. He even came down to my office to get more medicine, to save me a trip, and said everything was coming along fine.

"That horse was a champion hunter in Ireland. There wasn't any reason for him to act as though he'd never seen a jump before," he concluded as though puzzled.

"If Red's too busy to take care of the horse, maybe now you can help," he said.

"Oh, yes, that's what I plan to do," Rosemary answered eagerly, trying to forget the warning Don and Steve had given her.

Dr. Potter explained the necessity for keeping the

wound clean and told her what medications to use. Before she left his office, he said, "Let me know if you want me to come out and see the horse. Don't hesitate to call if there's anything I can do."

It had been so comforting to talk to him, she thought, still staring blankly at the wall. She hadn't exactly told him how bad she thought Irish was. . . . She wouldn't really know until she took off the bandages.

She wished Don and Steve would go home. She pulled her schedule out of the middle drawer of the desk for want of something to do and wondered if Red had written down any information as to how he wanted the horses worked. If he was going to be gone the whole week-end, there would be plenty to do.

The first few days she had worked at the stables, she'd had a hard time trying to figure out Red's routine. She knew he put the hounds out in runs and cleaned the kennels. Then he exercised them with a member of the hunt staff and fed them. Beyond that nothing was ever done the same way twice.

He would wait until she started to clean tack to tell her to take a class already waiting in the ring. He never let her know which horses he wanted ridden or which ones worked on a longe line. When she looked for a horse she had worked the day before, she would find it had been turned out in a paddock.

She thought about how much time she wasted looking for Red so she could ask him a question. Then she came up with her "schedules." She drew squares on a sheet of paper, listed the names of the horses in the first column and the days of the week across the top of the paper.

After that she decided on the symbols: "O" would

mean the owner was to ride; "P" would mean that the horse was to be turned out in the paddock; "R" would indicate that Rosemary would exercise the horse; and "RS" that Red was going to do the schooling.

Red's reaction had been far from encouraging. At first he looked at the schedule in surprise. Then he gave a grunt that was supposed to be a laugh, she guessed, changed his mind and said, "I don't have time to fool around with the alphabet," as he pushed the paper away.

"But we could *save* time. . . ." Rosemary started. She tried again. "Please, Red, I'll fill it out if you just tell me what to put down. Please?"

"Aw—" he gave an exaggerated sigh, as though he were being asked to do more than should be required of any human. Finally she got some of the squares filled in. But by the end of the day, she found she had worked more horses than appeared on her schedule. When Don saw what she was trying to do, he said, "You'll never get Red to go along with you on that!"

Maybe the schedule was a stupid idea, Rosemary thought. Maybe Don and Red were right, but her curiosity finally made her ask, "Why?"

"Well, for one thing, you're asking him to put down in writing just how much work he's getting you to do. When you're here Red doesn't do anything but the hound work and take his private pupils—like Billy. Wait 'til you're here every day—you'll be doing *all* of Red's work. And he isn't going to let that show on a chart. You'll see."

It was very discouraging, she thought. But she'd have to do the best she could. She put her blank schedule back in the desk and went out to help Don and Steve bring the horses in from the paddock. Finally everything was done and they were ready to leave, their work for the day finished.

Rosemary watched Don's convertible disappear around a bend in the road and heard the wheels of the car bump across the wooden bridge. The sound was no louder than the pounding of her heart.

She ran to the medicine cabinet, took out what she wanted, and filled a clean bucket with warm water. She put everything down carefully outside Irish's stall and reached for the door with hands that trembled. Why should she feel so guilty, she asked herself? She wasn't going to steal him!

She opened the top half of the door quietly and saw only an empty stall! Frightened, she raised herself on tip-toe and leaned over to look in.

Irish was down—maybe dead. He looked so crumpled up, so small and vulnerable. Her horrified eyes traveled from his head to his side. Was there any sign of breathing? She couldn't be sure. She opened the bottom half of the door with fingers that were stiff and clumsy.

Kneeling beside the horse, she put her hand out slowly and gently. He was warm—he was alive. But just barely!

She ran down the aisle to phone Dr. Potter. He wasn't in his office; the stereotyped voice of the answering service informed her that she could leave a message. Rosemary could have screamed while she waited for the mechanical voice to finish.

Instead, she forced herself to try to think calmly. What could she do for Irish while she waited for Dr. Potter? She could try to get him up—but how could she make him *stay* up? She remembered something she'd seen her father do long ago.

She ran up the narrow stairs to the hay loft. She'd have to get a bale of hay down to his stall, but it was too big to go through the overhead feed door. She looked at the wide, double doors through which the hay was brought up by pulleys and rope, threw the doors open and turned to the nearest bale.

She pulled and tugged, tried rolling it over and over. No matter how she did it, it was slow work. The hay cut her hands but she barely noticed. She used hay hooks. Little by little, she got it to the door and pushed it out.

Now she needed something to cover the hay with. It was too scratchy. She grabbed a soft woolen blanket from the tackroom, threw it over the bale, and started dragging it again.

When she got the hay to Irish's stall, she straightened her stiff back, brushed the loose hair out of her eyes, and looked in. He was still in the same position in which she'd left him. She took his halter and rope off the hook on the wall and knelt down beside him.

Leaning over until her mouth was close to his face, she whispered, "Irish, if you get up I'll make you more comfortable. You're going to have to help, though. I can't get you up by myself. I brought a bale of hay so your poor, tired legs won't have to hold you up. We'll let the hay do some of the work. And maybe Dr. Potter will bring a sling for you. Please, Irish, please!"

She kissed him in the hollow above his eye, petted him gently on his face and neck, smoothed his mane. Tears were falling so fast she could hardly see. She lifted

96

his head to put his halter on and pulled on the shank. There was no flicker of life.

"Irish, I can't get you up by myself. You've got to help, please!" She put her arm around his flank, coaxing, pleading, encouraging. Her hands were everywhere—touching, urging. She looked at his head to see if there was the slightest sign that he heard her. Inwardly, she was in despair, outwardly she kept imploring the Irish horse to try.

She thought she saw a tiny movement of his ears, just the slightest bit. She held her breath, wiping at her eyes so her vision would be clear. At last he gave a tentative answer that was more a movement of his nostrils than a sound. His head raised slightly. Rosemary pulled his legs out in front of him.

His labored breathing sounded like sobs, his groans were piteous. She tried not to hear as she helped him up, pulling with all her might on the halter shank. The blanket was smooth over the bale and the hay was pushed under him with her last bit of strength.

She sponged his eyes and nostrils gently and he made a small movement of his lips. She carried fresh water to him but he only took a sip.

It seemed to Rosemary that she stood beside Irish for hours and hours, watching the shadows lengthen through the open door. She talked to him and was silent. She was sure he liked to be petted. She could see his ears relax a little.

When it was almost dark in his stall, she heard a car clank across the bridge.

"Hello? Anybody here?" Dr. Potter called.

97

"I'm in the stall," Rosemary answered. "The light switch is on the left of the door to the office."

"I'll find it and be with you in a minute."

Dr. Potter's keen eyes took in everything in one quick glance. "Did you get him up and that thing under him all by yourself?"

She could only nod. Her throat felt raw and thick.

"You did a fine job." He opened his black bag and drew out bottles and a hypodermic needle.

Rosemary allowed herself one blissful moment to relax and then said, "I haven't called home. My aunt and uncle will think something's happened to me. Excuse me while I phone."

She ran to the office and dialed. With a sigh of relief she heard Bruce's voice answer. He wouldn't ask any questions or be critical.

Dr. Potter was undoing the crusted bandages carefully when she returned. "Where's Red?" he asked.

"He's down south looking at horses."

Dr. Potter raised his eyebrows. "From the looks of this bandage, it apparently doesn't matter whether Red's here or down south.

"Tell me—are you going to work every day now that school is out?"

"Yes," Rosemary answered.

"You'll be able to help with this horse then." He looked at her. "You want to, don't you?"

"Oh, yes, more than anything else. But . . ." and then she told Dr. Potter what Don had said about Red's strict orders.

Dr. Potter was silent as he sponged the gaping wound

98

now exposed. Rosemary had to grit her teeth and clench her hands before she could look at it.

"How did you get your job, Rosemary?"

She explained about Mr. Medford hiring her the day of the hunter trials.

"Good enough. He hired you so if anyone is going to fire you—it should be Mr. Medford. And he's not even here now. He's back east. Try not to let Red catch you working on the horse; but that's an 'out' if he does. You're not afraid of him like those kids, are you?"

"No, I'm not afraid of him. I'm just afraid Irish might die!"

"Rosemary, do you know what TLC is?"

She shook her head. "No."

"It's an expression they use in hospitals. It's worth more than any medicine known to man and it will do more than the skill of the finest doctor. TLC means tender, loving care. That's what will pull this horse through.

"I tried to tell Red that—not quite in the same way. The horse had the will to live. If he hasn't lost it, and I don't think he has, he needs lots of TLC, tender, loving care. So it's up to you. Can you do it?"

"Oh, I will. Of course, I will, Dr. Potter. I'll do anything so he won't die. I promise."

Dr. Potter patted her on her arm. "I know you will. If there's any real trouble, I'll talk to Mr. Medford when he comes back, but I'd rather not. He's put Red in charge of the stables and trusts him implicitly.

"You see, Mr. Medford has so many businesses and so many interests and projects—horses too for that matter

99

—scattered all over, he has to trust people to do their jobs. He can't concern himself with every detail."

Dr. Potter went to his car and came back with a sling, a hammock-like contraption, and ropes. He put screw hooks in the ceiling, made adjustments, and showed her how the sling worked as Irish was carefully and slowly suspended in it.

"This will give his legs a rest. Put him in it as often as you can."

They dragged the bale of hay into the stall next door. Rosemary swept the aisle.

"Better let me give you a ride home," Dr. Potter said. "You must be pretty tired."

He hoisted her bicycle into the back of his station wagon.

Before she got out of his car, he said, "You know, I think that Irish horse is lucky after all."

She looked at him aghast. She couldn't believe her ears. "Lucky?"

"Yes," he said with a smile. "Finally—he's found an Irish friend."

Rosemary smiled weakly. "I think maybe he's found *two* friends."

10. *Hound Exercise*

By the time Don and Steve came to work the next morning, Rosemary was feeding horses.

She'd already cleaned out Irish's stall clear to the bottom, put lime down, and brought in fresh bedding. She'd made him a bran mash, given him his medication, sponged his face, and checked for signs of rubbing from the sling.

She was sure his eyes were brighter. He had seemed happy to see her. Her heart sang! She planned to change his bandages after Don and Steve left at the end of the day.

Rosemary told Don he wouldn't have to feed the Irish

horse in Red's absence. She would do it. He nodded without saying anything.

Although there were hounds to be taken care of, in addition to the other work, everything went smoothly. All the jobs were shared.

Rosemary could hear Steve whistling at the other end of the barn. Don was up at the kennels. Even the horses, chomping on the last of their hay, making sucking sounds as they drank water, or rustling bedding as they shifted position in their stalls, sounded contented. She wished it were this way all the time.

At ten o'clock the phone rang. Running to answer, Rosemary was slightly breathless as she said, "Fallow Field Stables."

"Hello, Rosemary? This is Mrs. Randolph. I'm supposed to exercise hounds today and can't find a soul to go out with me. Is there anyone available at the stables?"

"There's no one here now except the boys and me," Rosemary explained, "and there's only a children's class scheduled for this afternoon."

"You've never gone out with hounds, have you?" Mrs. Randolph asked.

"No, I haven't."

"Do you want to give it a try? Are you very busy?"

"No, I'm not too busy," Rosemary answered, not quite truthfully. "I only have one class and some horses to ride." She quickly decided she could pony a few of the horses and turn the rest of them out. After all, hound exercise was terribly important.

"Well—you'll get one horse exercised going out with hounds. I'll be right over. And thanks, dear."

Mrs. Randolph must be the owner of Champ, the

horse Cindy had ridden, Rosemary thought. And the owner of the outside course she and Mr. Sedgwick jumped.

She certainly didn't waste any time getting to the stables, Rosemary decided, as she watched a small, gray-haired woman on a workmanlike bay gelding ride up to the archway. She tossed her reins to Steve, flashed him a quick smile, and came into the stables with a purposeful look in her eye.

"I've heard so much about you, I feel I know you already," she said warmly to Rosemary. "Even Ben mentioned you—and he thinks the last good rider was lost when my daughter went away to college."

She selected couplings and a hunting whip from the tackroom. "Have you ever used one of these, Rosemary?" she asked and with a small movement of her wrist, the lash of the whip flicked a corner of the dust cover on a saddle.

Rosemary could feel her mouth open in surprise. She closed it and shook her head in awe. "The only time I held one was when I rode in teams at the hunter trials."

"That's a shame. Drat that Red anyway. He doesn't bother checking with anyone—just considers his own plans." She looked at Rosemary searchingly.

"Something tells me you might as well learn this job the right way—and thoroughly. I'm beginning to think you'll be doing it a lot this summer and there's no way to learn to use a hunting whip except by practicing. And more practicing!

"Carry it with you whenever you ride a horse. Take it home with you tonight and practice. You won't get

103

the same effect but it will help a little. Well—we'll leave the puppies home today and hope for the best.

"What horse are you planning to ride?" Mrs. Randolph asked.

Rosemary told her she had already tacked up Fair Kate, the big chestnut mare Red used on the hunt.

"Good. She'll teach you half your job. Let's get started, Rosemary."

She didn't understand everything Mrs. Randolph said. She would have to watch her every minute and learn to use the hunting whip as fast as she could. She held the whip as she'd seen Mrs. Randolph do and tried a tentative movement of her wrist.

On leaving the kennels, the hounds seemed to know exactly what was required of them. It almost seemed too easy, Rosemary thought. Mrs. Randolph was worried and she didn't impress Rosemary as a person who would worry for no reason.

She tried to imitate Mrs. Randolph's voiced commands and her movements with the hunting whip but she didn't think she was fooling the hounds one bit. They knew she didn't know what she was doing. She could tell by the way they lifted their heads and looked at her so searchingly. They were as puzzled as she was. She hoped she wouldn't be the cause of any trouble. What was Mrs. Randolph thinking, she wondered, with the responsibility of the whole pack on her slight shoulders.

The hounds' behavior was wonderful as they went down the road and cut into a field, following a wide trail that was partly a fire break and partly a riding path.

104

Mrs. Randolph seemed to relax a little. "I wasn't here for the hunter trials," she said, "but I understand Cindy Sedgwick did a good job on our old chestnut horse. Do you like to teach, Rosemary?"

"Oh, yes," she answered, trying to relax a little herself.

"We're lucky to have you at the stables. I can see that already. You'll probably have a few of the youngsters ready for shows this summer.

"The only thing, dear," Mrs. Randolph continued in a kindly voice, "don't let them work you too hard. Red has a tremendous knowledge of horses and hounds and none at all about people." She shook her head sadly. "He doesn't seem to want to use his knowledge any more. He lost interest a long time ago. However, Mr. Medford is still satisfied and it really isn't any of my business. The only reason I mention it is that I don't like to see a young girl overworked. You're liable to grow to hate horses—or get sick—or both."

"Oh, no, I won't," Rosemary protested. "I'd never hate horses. Don't worry. And I won't get sick either. I know I'm kind of thin and I haven't grown for a long time but I'm stronger than I look and I'm never sick. Really. But it's nice of you to worry."

Mrs. Randolph smiled and changed the subject. She talked about the horse shows that the hunt members attended in the summer—the ones that put emphasis on cross-country classes rather than open jumping. "And then, of course," she finished, "everyone goes to Eric Calhoun's three-day show at Indian Creek.

"Maybe you can get a good rest when that's over, Rosemary. Eric's show is the first week-end in August.

105

After that everyone disappears for the rest of the month —Tahoe and so on. And some of us are going to see the Dublin Show. I suggest you sleep late when we're all gone and turn everybody's horse out."

Rosemary didn't pay much attention to Mrs. Randolph's suggestion. Her mind was fixed on what she had said just before that. "Did you say you were going to the *Dublin* Horse Show? In Ireland?"

Mrs. Randolph laughed. "That's right—the Dublin, Ireland, Horse Show."

"Oh!" Rosemary couldn't say any more.

Mrs. Randolph looked at her questioningly. Rosemary felt she had to come up with something. "It's just that —well—" She swallowed. "The only real relative I have in the whole world—my uncle—" her voice faded. Mrs. Randolph wouldn't be interested.

But apparently Mrs. Randolph was interested. Before long Rosemary was telling her about her father's younger brother, Sean O'Connor, who had a wife and children and worked in a stable that raised hunters for the show ring and hunting field, near Dublin.

Then they came to the end of the field in which they had been riding. Mrs. Randolph had to choose between a busy highway and a narrow road with houses on either side. She chose the narrow road.

Rosemary tried to help guide the hounds, feeling useless. The pleasant glow—when Mrs. Randolph had shown so much interest in Uncle Sean and promised to look him up if she had time—faded.

The hounds were once again in some kind of order. Rosemary relaxed a little, patting Fair Kate on the neck for being such a knowing horse. The mare knew better than Rosemary which way she should go to keep hounds in the pack.

Just as Rosemary was wondering if Mrs. Randolph would tell her more about the Dublin Show, a black flash of fur hurled itself at the center of the pack. Out of nowhere, a middle-sized poodle had burst into view, bent on taking on the whole pack of hounds.

With horn, whip, and voice, Mrs. Randolph worked to draw the hounds off. Rosemary had never felt so helpless. Not all the hounds were obeying Mrs. Randolph. They'd kill the poodle if she didn't do something quick.

She jumped off Fair Kate and directed a silent prayer to the chestnut mare to be good. Throwing the reins over a protruding pomegranate branch, she flew to the center of the pack, trying to use her whip. The yelping poodle and excited hounds almost deafened her.

She had the poodle's collar in her hand when the front door of the house in front of her opened and a sharp, male voice called, "Charles de Gaulle! Get in here this minute!" Like a streak in the wake of a meteor, the poodle was away, seeming to fly over the pack and into the house. The slamming door startled even the hounds.

"Get on forward," Rosemary tried to keep her voice from shaking. Using her hunting whip as well as she knew how, she forced them to move on.

"Good girl," Mrs. Randolph said when Rosemary drew up to her. Mrs. Randolph was expertly gathering up the last hound in the pack. She called them by name as she scolded. Rosemary wondered if she would ever be as knowing about hounds as Mrs. Randolph.

"I'm sorry I wasn't any help," she said. "If you'll let me come with you again, maybe I can learn."

"You have courage, dear, and that's something you don't just learn, like popping a hunting whip. Drat— now I'll have to stop at that house and calm down the owner of the poodle." She gave a sigh.

"Individually, hounds have the sweetest disposition in the world," Mrs. Randolph said a moment later. "They're affectionate—timid—but in a pack they're hunters."

"That wouldn't have happened if you'd had someone with you who could have given you some real help," Rosemary said, feeling guilty.

"Maybe it wouldn't have happened—and maybe it would. Their instincts—don't worry about it, dear. You did very well."

The hounds were subdued going home and Rosemary breathed a sigh of relief to see them safely in their kennels. Mrs. Randolph showed her some books in the office about hunting and hounds and told her to take them home to read. They would be very helpful in teaching her to understand hounds.

Rosemary went out with Mrs. Randolph for the three days that Red was gone and learned to put enough authority in her voice so that the hounds obeyed when she cried "Have a care." Using her hunting whip effectively, she realized, was going to take a lot longer.

Red hadn't come back from down south by the time Rosemary was ready to go home on Sunday. She knew

108

she was taking a chance, but she left Irish in the sling.

At the stables early Monday morning, he looked so much better she decided to leave him as he was until she saw Red's car coming up the road. But during lunch hour, she lost her courage and took the sling off, putting it in the empty stall next door, behind some large tackboxes that were used only at the bigger shows.

She massaged Irish's legs to get the circulation back and bathed the injured leg in warm water and Epsom salts until her hands turned purplish-white and were so puckered and wrinkled they made her laugh. Irish was better; his eyes followed her as she worked. He even sniffed at the palm of her hand once.

She cut fresh alfalfa, hand-feeding it to him. She bet herself anything he nickered at her. She hadn't quite heard him but she saw his nostrils flutter.

She had fed, watered, bathed, cleaned, rubbed, massaged, petted him—she ticked them off on her fingers—yes, and prayed over him. It didn't matter now if Red neglected him because tomorrow she'd do the same and the day after the same and the day after that.

Dr. Potter had said he was a champion hunter in Ireland. She could see how this was so as far as his conformation was concerned. His bone structure was wonderful. When his ribs were covered, his flanks filled out. . . . She half-closed her eyes to look at him. His poor neck was awfully thin now but his head was beautiful. She mentally added weight to his neck, his top line, a sheen to his coat, dapples to his flanks. . . . Oh! She could hardly wait until she had him looking like that again!

Red was suddenly back, breaking the quiet of the past

few days, "Wanna see the horse I bought? He's a full brother to Billy Medford's horse. Bet you can't tell 'em apart."

"Bet I can," Rosemary said under her breath. But she went to look anyway.

11. *"Cubbing"*

Rosemary smiled impartially at the small boys on either side of her as they brought their horses down to a walk and a rest. They had just galloped on a wide trail, shaded by an occasional bay tree, clumps of redwoods and pines.

Billy Medford, on her left, was riding his horse, Indian Summer, the stodgy chestnut he'd shown in the hunter trials. His two friends, Richie and Mark, rode on her left.

Ahead of them, five little girls loosened their reins without being told and the braver ones took their feet out of the stirrups. The jingle of metal as the stirrups tangled made them giggle. Billy caught Rosemary's eye and gestured with his hand to show their lack of brains.

His horse brushed against hers. She looked down to see why Indian Summer was crowding and saw Billy urging him over in a fair two-track. He grinned at her and said, "Gosh, Rosie, I'm glad Dad lets me come out on the cubbing rides now. This is sure lots more fun than riding around and around in an old ring."

"I'm glad, too, Billy." And it's lots more fun for me, she told herself.

Rosemary and Mrs. Randolph had thought of the picnic rides for the children on one of the first days they had exercised hounds together. Mrs. Randolph knew from long experience that "riding with a purpose," as she called it, would keep the younger ones more interested.

Only Rosemary called the picnic rides "cubbing" rides, from something she had learned in one of the hunting books she read. She knew she wasn't using the word properly but she liked to interpret it in her own way. The children loved to call it cubbing; it made them feel important. So the picnic rides were cubbing rides and they "met" every Monday and Thursday and their "season" was all of vacation.

Today was one of the best rides they'd had so far. No one had been frightened—nor had anyone fallen off. Although they were all relaxed in their saddles, they didn't slouch. They were learning fast, Rosemary thought with pride, as she looked at each of them.

Her eyes stopped at Billy. His improvement gave her the most satisfaction even though it always reminded her of the awful scene she'd witnessed between Red and Mr. Medford.

112

Billy had asked and asked Red to be allowed to go on the cubbing rides. Sometimes she had heard them talking and sometimes Billy had told her about it. Red always said Billy wasn't a good enough rider and that he was responsible for him. Then Billy would say that if Rosemary could be responsible for all the other children, why couldn't she be responsible for him, too?

This always made Red angry at Rosemary. She could tell when Billy spoke to Red by the way he treated her afterward.

Finally Mr. Medford had come home from one of his many business trips and Billy told him about the cubbing rides and asked if he couldn't ride on them.

Rosemary shuddered remembering the day Mr. Medford stalked into the stables, calling for Red. She was cleaning tack right next door to the office and tried to get away. But Mr. Medford called her into the office, too.

He asked her about the rides, what she did and how the children got along. With Red glowering at her, she explained about the follow-the-leader game they played —down banks, through streams, over creaking bridges, and the gallops they had on the flat.

"Well—what's the matter with that, Red?" Mr. Medford asked. Without waiting for an answer, he continued, "Sounds like Rosemary's getting them ready for the hunting field. As a matter of fact, it sounds like something a sedentary adult like me ought to be encouraged to try."

"Billy's not ready for it," Red said. "An accident would ruin him for horses for the rest of his life," he finished in a confident tone.

113

"Rosemary!" Mr. Medford's voice was sharp. "Tell me who some of the children are who go on the rides with you."

Rosemary swallowed hard and wet her lips. "There's Gia and Brooke Hanlon, Patsey Hughes and, uh, Richie Tupper, Mark Sanderson. . . ."

Mr. Medford exploded! "If those kids—who don't know one end of a horse from another—can go, why can't Billy?" He sounded as though he'd been insulted. "Sometimes I can't figure you out, Red!

"Keep on giving the boy lessons, but let him ride with the other children whenever he wants. If he has an accident, it'll be *my* responsibility." With a nod of dismissal, he reached for the phone and started to dial. The whole unpleasant scene was forgotten as far as he was concerned.

"Which way do we go now?" Brooke Hanlon, a nine-year-old girl with freckles and mischievous blue eyes turned in her saddle to ask. Rosemary was glad to put the incident of Mr. Medford out of her mind.

"To the left," she called. "I have something new for you to try today. Maybe I'd better lead the way."

She trotted ahead. As she caught up with the first rider, she said, "Gather up your reins, feet in the stirrups, and get ready to trot."

She moved on to get them started and then dropped back so she could watch without having to turn around. Even the smallest child, Pete Hughes' sister, Patsey, was sitting firmer in the saddle, she thought. More than anything else, she was pleased that they were willing to try something new. They might still forget to keep their heels down and their shoulders back now and then. But

114

they never wrapped their legs around their horses' barrels, nor tried to hang on by the reins, as they had done before, when they were presented with a new obstacle.

"We turn here," Rosemary indicated, and a moment later signalled for them to stop.

They were at an abandoned quarry she had found one day when she was giving one of the younger horses a long work-out.

"Today we graduate to this beautiful slide," she said, pointing to a sharp, rocky incline. "I want you to go up one at a time. Then you can come back down. Remember! When you go up, lean forward to help your horse pull himself up. When you come down, sit up straighter so that if your horse decides to play, you don't get pitched over his head. *And keep your heels down.*

"I'll go first so you can see it's not too hard and then, Gia—you lead off."

Rosemary and her horse started up. She let him choose his way and, with powerful thrusts of his hindquarters, he soon reached the top. Coming down, she restrained him but didn't try to prevent his eager jump down to the flat ground as he neared the end of the slide.

One of the girls squealed, half in fear and half in delight. "Are all the horses going to jump like that?" Patsey Hughes asked, her voice shaky.

"Can we jump, too, Rosie?" Billy wanted to know.

"It will be almost impossible to keep them from jumping," Rosemary said. "Just don't let any of them get their heads down."

They nodded in solemn agreement. At one time or another they had all had their horses suddenly lower

115

their heads and give a few playful bucks. And a few of them had taken a spill or two. They wouldn't forget.

"All right, Gia. It's your turn."

Gia, a year older than her sister, Brooke, was proud to be chosen first and determined to do well. She leaned so far forward, her chest touched her horse's neck.

One after the other the children helped their horses up the steep hill by not hindering them.

After the last horse reached the top, Rosemary said, "Fine! I don't have one bit of criticism to make. Now, you can come back and, this time, Brooke can lead. Remember, sit up straight and keep more feel on your horse's mouth."

She could see the set looks on their faces, the doggedness with which they were tackling the almost straightdown descent. She had a word of encouragement for each one of them. The horses that jumped at the bottom of the slide were pulled up before they became too exuberant.

Every face shone with pride and satisfaction when it was over. They didn't need Rosemary's congratulations to tell them they had done well. They had ridden their horses up and back successfully and they were all determined to recount exactly how it felt every scary step of the way.

They wouldn't have heard if she did try to say something, she thought. The chatter was deafening. She smiled as she listened to them, feeling as though she were a million years older than they.

And that reminded her of Cindy's new seriousness when she rode with Rosemary to help watch out for the

116

cubbers. Cindy loved the responsibility and acted so grown-up.

If more than eight or nine children signed up for the ride, Rosemary felt better if she had another experienced rider along. Pete had come out with the cubbers once when he was home from Echo Lake on his day off. He was working at the lake as "boat boy" because, as he said, it was the only way he could get as much water skiing as he liked. He sent her a postcard now and then with a few words scrawled on the back which she always had trouble deciphering.

Sometimes Debbie or Anne Medford rode with her when they were home and not at Tahoe or Santa Barbara. They were down south now but before they left, Debbie made a special trip to the stables with the trunk of her car filled with boxes for Rosemary.

"Anne and I have outgrown everything in there," she had said, pointing. "Mostly it's riding clothes and boots but there are a few other things, too.

"We're glad to get rid of them," she said, brushing aside Rosemary's thanks, "so we can get some new clothes."

Even now Rosemary was wearing beautifully-cut jodhpurs and hand-made paddock shoes. She wriggled her toes with pleasure as she looked at them. All she had to do now was to figure out where she could wear a silk organza dress with lovely red roses etched on it.

Rosemary led the noisy, now ragged column towards the picnic site by the creek. She tried to vary the route each time she took the cubbers out. Whatever place she chose for lunch had to be negotiable for the pick-up

117

truck so Don could be there ahead of them with the food and halters for the horses.

Each child brought a lunch from home. Don brought cartons of milk from the store and ropes to make a picket line for the horses.

The cubbers took care of their own horses at the picnic grounds. They loosened saddles, put halters on, watered their mounts at the creek and tied them safely to the picket line, constructed of ropes wrapped around trees.

"Rosie—" Billy was tugging on her sleeve. "My Dad's coming out to watch me ride tomorrow afternoon. Will you watch, too?"

"I sure will. Won't *you* have a surprise for him?"

"Yeah." Billy leaned back against her arm and looked dreamily towards the creek as though he were already enjoying his father's surprise.

Rosemary herself was still surprised at how fast Billy had improved once he'd started riding with the cubbers. She looked down at his curly black head and snub nose and suddenly wished she had a small brother exactly like him. She wondered if he'd be embarrassed if she hugged him. Probably.

12. *From Bad to Worse*

· The happy hours Rosemary spent with the children twice a week on the cubbing rides made the atmosphere in the stables drearier than ever. She never heard Steve whistle at his work any more and when the children were gone there was never any laughter.

She could almost feel the tension as she walked into the stables each morning. Gloomy day succeeded gloomy day. The dull, gnawing ache about Irish never let up.

He didn't go down in his stall again but the process of healing was so slow she sometimes thought it was at a standstill. Although he now ate well, it would be a long time before his ribs were covered and his hindquarters filled out. Dr. Potter had said something about

119

osteomyelitis. Supposing the bone in his leg was affected?

Rosemary came to the stables earlier in the morning and stayed later and later in the afternoon. She never took a day off and didn't really need an excuse for coming back, for no provision for doing her work while she was gone was suggested.

Red always went to town for lunch. Sometimes he didn't return. If he did, he would get cleaned up and leave again as soon as the last rider was gone.

When he remembered to do something for Irish, it was in the morning. Then he left him alone for the rest of the day. So Rosemary cleaned Irish's stall at noon and changed his bandages and gave him a bran mash at night.

Once when she went into Irish's stall in the late afternoon and saw him blink at the light that came in from the open door, she couldn't stand it any more. He should have fresh air and sunshine. He could bear weight on his injured leg now.

She took him out of the stall and it hurt her to see him blink his eyes again in the still bright sunshine and look around as though he were in a strange place. How long had it been since he'd seen the sun, she wondered? His ears signalled all sorts of messages. Then he'd looked at her for reassurance. He might as well be asking, "Are you sure it's all right for me to be out here?"

She walked him over to the alfalfa patch and recklessly let him crop some of the succulent green leaves. Just as she was leading him back to the stables, she got caught!

Mr. Sedgwick, on Understudy, was right in front of

120

her! She hadn't even heard him. She tried to quiet her pounding heart by telling herself better Mr. Sedgwick than Red—but it didn't help. The idea that anyone could arrive so quietly, without her hearing, was scary. Mr. Sedgwick looked serious. His first question took her by surprise.

"Do you always work this late, Rosemary?"

"No," she answered. After all, what she was doing wasn't *work.*

"Does Red make you take care of Dublin Jack?"

Rosemary wet her lips. She didn't know how to explain—but Mr. Sedgwick always had been easy to talk to. In a way it would be a relief to tell him everything.

She started at the beginning, when she'd gone to Irish's stall the first time, and the condition he was in. She told him about the week-end when Red had been down south, about calling Dr. Potter—everything.

Mr. Sedgwick looked shocked the whole time she talked, and terribly serious and stern. "Did Red ever say anything directly to you about Dublin Jack?" he asked finally.

She shook her head. "All I know is what Don and Steve told me—and that isn't very much. I had to ask and ask before they'd tell me anything."

"I'm afraid they're right about Red's reaction to anyone going against his orders."

Rosemary looked down at her clenched hands. "I'm sorry, Mr. Sedgwick, but don't tell me not to take care of Irish. I love him more than any horse I've known in my whole life. But even if I didn't, I couldn't let any horse that needed help be neglected. And—and—and I'm *not* going to let Red destroy him!"

She burst into tears.

When she could control herself enough to look at Mr. Sedgwick, she saw that he looked worried, but not shocked at what she had said. He held out his handkerchief.

"Rosemary, I've been hearing a lot of stories about Red—from reliable sources—and none of them good. He's been seen a lot at the tavern in town, late at night. And we know he's not doing his job here. I'm afraid. . . . Don't. . . ." He tried again. "Sometimes I'm sorry I got you involved in this." He shook his head sadly.

"Unfortunately, as you probably know, Mr. Medford is in Europe now. If you can hold out until he comes back, we'll talk to him. He'll have to be told now.

"Don't worry about Dublin Jack, or Irish as you call him. Red won't do anything to him now. If he'd wanted to destroy him, he could have in the very beginning. Just be careful—and stay out of his way as much as possible."

He watched as she put Irish in his stall and didn't get back on Understudy until she had her bicycle out of the rack and waved good-bye.

At least Mr. Sedgwick hadn't tried to make her promise not to stay so late, Rosemary thought with relief. She felt better now that she had confided in someone. As stern as Mr. Sedgwick's face was when she talked to him, she was sure he didn't entirely disapprove of what she was doing.

The next morning early, Red drove away in his car without a word to anyone. The boys cleaned the kennels and Mrs. Randolph and Rosemary exercised hounds. She could flick her hunting whip at a blade of grass now

122

and tear it neatly down the middle, but her skill gave her no pleasure. Mrs. Randolph looked grim and had little to say and Rosemary retired into her own melancholy thoughts.

After they brought the hounds back, she saw Mrs. Randolph talking to the boys. Later they said she suggested they keep halters on all the horses in the stalls. Rosemary suspected she had said more than that—at least she must have given a reason for the request. But the boys didn't say any more. Don just looked grim, like Mrs. Randolph.

The boys hesitated to go to town for lunch because they said they didn't want to leave Rosemary at the stables alone. It wasn't until she offered to take her sandwich and exercise one of the horses out on the trail that they left.

Rosemary had barely picked up her lunch in its paper sack and started towards the tackroom when she heard a car. It sounded like Red's battered hardtop. She ducked into a stall quickly so he wouldn't see her, the boys' concern suddenly making her afraid. She could hear Red go into the office and the scrape of the chair as he sat down.

Well—she couldn't stay in the stall forever. She let herself out quietly and started towards Irish. Red would hear if she tried to take a horse out now. Besides, she didn't want to leave Irish. She nibbled at her sandwich, sitting in the archway by his stall. Now and then she could hear him switch his tail. Once she heard him give a long sigh. Her heart contracted.

Poor Irish! It was worse than being in jail—it was

like being in solitary confinement. And what was he being punished for?

Did he wonder, when he heard footsteps, if someone were coming to free him at least? He hardly knew day from night. He never saw the sun shine, never heard birds sing, nor felt a soft breeze ruffle his mane. . . .

How long had the telephone been ringing, she wondered? Well, Red could answer it; he was sitting right next to it. But it continued to ring. She guessed Red had gone to his apartment. He wouldn't hear it in there. Reluctantly she put her unfinished sandwich back in its paper sack and slowly walked towards the office. The closer she got, the more her steps lagged.

She stopped in the open doorway and her heart sank. She was looking straight at Red! He was still sitting at the desk. He had a cigarette in his mouth and was holding a glass in his hand and starting to reach for a bottle with his other hand when he saw her. He changed his mind and picked up the telephone.

"H'lo," he said indistinctly into the phone without removing his cigarette. "H'lo?" He tried to put the receiver back, missed, and tried again. "Nobody there," he mumbled.

Rosemary turned and ran. Now she knew what Mr. Sedgwick meant about Red's being in a tavern late at night.

After that, surprisingly, he seemed to pull himself together. He still neglected Irish, the boys did all the kennel work, but he exercised hounds more or less regularly. He suddenly lost interest in Billy and told

Rosemary to give him his lessons. He said it would be good experience for her.

She never did get to any of the promised horse shows. Red went to all of them, taking Don to drive the van and help with the horses. When the children came back with ribbons, Red boasted as though he had done all the teaching. The three-day show at Indian Creek came and went and Rosemary stayed at the stables exercising hounds and the horses that were left.

Then, without warning, she arrived at the stables one morning to find Irish's stall door wide open! Her knees buckled and she leaned against the wall for support.

Someone was yelling in a back paddock. Hanging on to the wall, she looked out and saw Red running. He was trying to catch—IRISH!

"Saints above!" Rosemary whispered as she watched in horror. Irish was trying to stay out of Red's reach. He ran awkwardly, his head bobbing with pain as he exerted pressure on his injured leg. Red swung the chain end of the lead line he carried and hit Irish on the flank— so hard she could hear the sound as the chain hit flesh and Irish's involuntary grunt. He squealed in pain, kicked out in protest, and almost fell. Red ducked and swore loudly.

Rosemary couldn't stand any more. She ran to the fence, not bothering with the gate, and crawled through. She gave a soft whistle as she straightened up. Irish stopped, turned, and nickered at her.

"No one is going to hurt you any more, Irish," she soothed as she walked up to him. She could hear his nervous breathing, could see the welt the chain had raised, the sweat that dripped from his stomach and his

125

flaring nostrils and wild eyes. "No one is going to hurt you again. I promise!"

"How long have you been fooling around with this horse?" Red asked, barring her way at the gate.

She didn't answer. Her legs were trembling and her heart was pounding. She was more frightened than she'd ever been before in her life but she wasn't going to let Red do anything more to Irish. She'd find the courage somehow. She tried to lead Irish forward.

Red still barred her way.

"You wanted to put him back in his stall, didn't you?" she asked finally, her voice quavering.

"I don't need any help from you," he said. "I was catching up horses before you were born!"

Rosemary saw the chain start to swing again. She reached for the bar on the gate, opened it, pushed, and Irish was on the other side as the chain flew through the air.

She had the brown gelding in his stall before Red caught up with her.

"You know this horse was going to be destroyed, don't you? He's no good," he said as he reached for the door.

Rosemary planted herself in front of Irish and held the door with both hands. "He's getting along fine and you know it! You can't destroy him now. You can't touch him until Mr. Medford comes home."

"We'll see if I have to wait for Mr. Medford," he threatened. "Do you know what we do with horses like him? Let me tell you how we do it. We . . ."

Rosemary couldn't stand any more. Her eyes blinded by tears, she let go of the door. Still protecting Irish

126

with her body, she pressed her hands hard against her ears to keep from hearing what Red was saying.

She didn't know how long she stood there. Irish's soft nose nuzzled her for attention and sympathy. She brought her hands down and put them around his neck. Red was gone but his words still rang loudly in her ears. "Let me tell you how we do it. We . . ."

She stayed close to Irish until Don and Steve came to work. For the rest of the day, as long as Red was in the stables, she was never far from the brown horse's stall.

Red left early in the afternoon and Rosemary stayed late. She called home when she was sure her aunt would be getting dinner and one of her cousins would answer the phone. When Joe was on the line, she told him she'd be late. He wasn't curious enough to ask why and she was glad she wouldn't have to lie.

At eight o'clock Red hadn't come back. If she stayed much longer it would be dark and her bike didn't have lights.

She pedalled home quickly, picked at her dinner, which had been kept warm in the oven, and rinsed her dish. Then she went to her room.

She was thankful her bedroom was off the back porch. She couldn't be heard once everyone settled down for the night. By ten o'clock the house was quiet. It was easy to slip out. She walked as fast as she could, taking shortcuts through fields, climbing fences and going around sleeping cattle in pastures.

Rosemary was on her way to the Fallow Field Stables to steal Irish!

13. A Thief in the Night

Rosemary had known, the minute she saw Red hit Irish with the chain, that she was going to have to steal him. She didn't need his threats to help her make up her mind and she didn't have to talk herself into it.

She had done a lot of things she shouldn't have and now she was going to do something much, much worse. She didn't know what the penalty was for stealing a horse and she didn't care!

She guessed she'd always had it in the back of her mind that some day she might have to steal him. Otherwise, why had she ridden so often past the abandoned farm on Spring Hill Road? She had looked in the barn one day, wondering if it was in any better condition than the house, which had all its windows broken. The doors in the barn still opened and closed. She'd seen buckets and there was well water.

As she neared the stables, she left the road and walked on the grass. It wouldn't do to kick a pebble with her boots. If she were careful, she wouldn't disturb the hounds. They were sort of far away from the stables anyway.

Red's car loomed up ahead. Just seeing the dusty, half-crumpled rear fender made her shiver. Well, she'd sort of expected he might be back. After all, it was about 10:30. He'd be in his apartment asleep. Irish's stall was at the other end of the stables. The tackroom was even farther away from the apartment and she could find her way around it blindfolded. She'd left a snaffle bit on top of her saddle and hay, tied in a gunny sack, in the un-used stall next to Irish. She hadn't made up her mind whether to walk or ride him but if she had any trouble, she could control him better with a bit in his mouth. Tomorrow, somehow, she'd have to buy some feed and take it to his new home.

She decided to go through the front archway and directly to the tackroom—then to the stall. She'd take one last look around and make sure everything was all right. Then she'd go in. She stopped and listened. The quiet was reassuring.

Nothing moved. There was not a whisper of a breeze and nothing stirred. The moon, high in the heavens, cast a friendly light. Everything was asleep. She breathed a small sigh of relief and took a step forward.

But she took only one step! She had seen a light in the office! Her heart started to pound. It must be Red—

what a narrow escape. But now she couldn't see it. Red must have turned the light off and left. Or had it been her imagination? She strained her eyes in the direction of the office and felt a dampness break out on her forehead. She saw it again. And then again there was no light.

Her eyes must be playing tricks on her. She looked away for a moment and then focused on the office. Now —there *was* a light! And then it disappeared.

Could someone be in the office using a flashlight? No, it wasn't like a flashlight—nor an electric light, either. And it wasn't her imagination!

The light was bright and then dim, and then brighter and brighter and bigger and bigger and the whole window was lit up—as though there was a huge flame behind it! It was a flame! The office was on fire! As she ran the reflection seemed to light up her path.

"Saints above! What shall I do?" Rosemary said aloud as she stopped in the doorway. By the light of the fire she saw Red sprawled across the desk.

The wastebasket, the long dusty drapes that reached from the ceiling to the floor, and part of the window frame were burning. A hundred thoughts seemed to race through her mind in a single instant—there was so much fire—it was too high up and travelling too fast for the fire extinguisher. She took a long, shuddering breath, coughed, and reached for the phone. Her hands seemed to function automatically. She'd have to call before the fire spread to the large desk. Then she had to get Red out of the office.

"Get the fire department," she said, when she had the operator. "This is Mr. Medford's stables on Horse Creek

Road, Las Parra. Hurry!" She hung up the receiver when she was sure the operator had the information and tried to pull Red out of the chair. She couldn't budge him and the straight chair wouldn't push. His dead weight was too much for her.

What about Irish, she thought with anguish? How long would it take the fire to race through the tackroom and the empty stalls? What about the horses on the other side of the archway? She could hear them, already whinnying in terror, stomping their feet and starting to pound against the walls. Fear spread through the stables faster than the flames. She thought she heard Irish give a shrill neigh.

Rosemary coughed again, gasped for breath, and with all her strength jerked Red's chair out from under him. He sprawled awkwardly on the floor. With the sound that might have been made by Irish still ringing in her ears, she pulled and then pushed, her eyes smarting, her breath labored. She tugged on Red's coat until she heard it tear and then grabbed his arm. She wouldn't have far to go, just out of the office, around the corner, and through the open archway. She mustn't listen to the crackle of flames nor the sounds the terrified horses made.

Finally Red was outside—she could go to Irish. But the fire was over the archway now and she'd have to do something about the horse in the first stall—Debbie Medford's gray mare, Miss America.

Gulping in great breaths of fresh air, she remembered, as though a million years before, Mrs. Randolph telling the boys to leave halters on the horses. Was this what she had been afraid of?

131

She took off her coat to use as a blindfold and reached for the halter shank on the wall as flames licked her fingers. She tried to talk to the gray mare to quiet her wild churning in the stall but it made her gag and she coughed harder. The smell of smoke was overpowering and the mare was frantic. She stepped on Rosemary, almost knocking her down. Finally she had the shank snapped to the mare's halter, her coat tied over her eyes. Gasping, choking, half-blind from the heat and smoke, Rosemary hung on to her with all her strength and pulled her out of the stall. They stumbled across the inner court yard, the mare either holding back or all but running Rosemary down. There were paddocks closer, she thought, but supposing the mare jumped out and went back into her stall. She would be safer in the high-fenced Hitchcock Pen and it was only a step or two further.

Then she heard the siren of the fire truck coming closer and closer. But Irish was calling, too. She could hear him. Would the driver of the fire truck see Red lying on the ground? And would the firemen know where to find the halter shanks and where to put the horses? Irish would have to wait a little bit longer.

She didn't have to explain anything; the firemen knew exactly what to do.

"You'd better take it easy now," one of them told her, his voice coming from far away. "Stay clear so you don't get hurt."

He didn't understand, Rosemary thought. How could he know that Irish was alone at the other end of the stables? She still had the gray mare's halter shank in her hand. Slowly, she went around the outside of the

132

stables. It was hard to make her legs move. They were heavy and, at the same time, so light she couldn't control them.

How had the fire spread so fast? She could hear Irish's ear-piercing scream of panic. He was trying to kick his way through the side of the stall, away from the fire. He couldn't hear her above the noise of the crackling flames and the toppling overhead timbers but she talked to him anyway, even though every word was painful. And now she didn't know what she was saying. It wouldn't matter if he'd only listen!

And then he did! He quieted down; only the trembling of his body, so intense it seemed to shake the earth beneath her feet, told her how frightened he was.

Suddenly she wasn't sure she could go any further. Her eyes streamed with burning tears; she couldn't see. She felt for the wall, the door, and staggered towards the archway, holding tight to Irish. She couldn't breathe. She could feel herself falling!

Irish would get away from her before she had him safely hidden in the abandoned barn. Irish must never go back into that stall again. Somehow, she felt a fence —a gate—she heard it slam.

He was safe now. Nobody would ever find him. She doubled over with searing pain and through burning, moisture-filled eyes, she saw as though from a great distance that . . . she . . . was . . . on . . . fire!

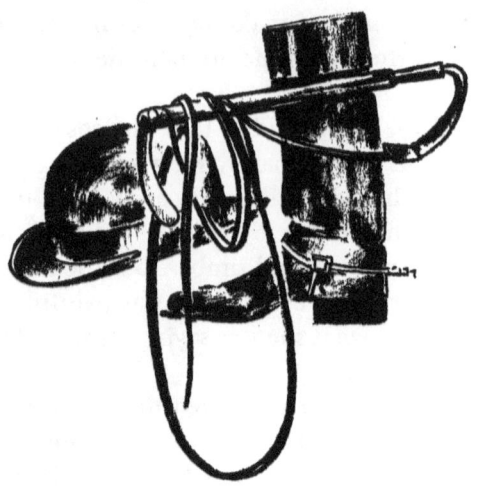

14. *Rosemary Comes Home*

For a long time Rosemary didn't know where she was. She felt as though she were suspended in space, floating on a sea of white clouds.

Lights would flash and bells ring in her ears so that she couldn't think and then she would float away again.

She tried to save Irish from the burning stables over and over, her legs heavy and sluggish and the brown horse just out of her reach. Sometimes she was with her mother and father, living in the trailer, listening to the rain beat on the roof. Then the rain changed to horses' hoofs, pounding on the stalls.

When she smelled flowers, she thought she was really

in heaven. As she tried to look around, the overhead timbers of the stables came crashing down. . . .

Rosemary awoke and knew where she was—finally. Woven through her consciousness, like a bright thread, were bits and pieces of reality. She could still see the burning stables when she closed her eyes; she would always hear the terrified whinnying of the horses, but now she remembered other things, too.

A parade of faces passed before her—of doctors and nurses. She could tell they were there without opening her eyes. The nurses rustled when they walked and the doctors had a special smell and there was always a lot of talk she couldn't remember because she'd fall asleep.

She thought her aunt and uncle had been in the room, too. And she faintly remembered seeing Bruce and Joe, looking strange and uncomfortable in their Sunday suits.

Mr. Sedgwick and Cindy had sat beside her. She was sure she'd seen them, but when she opened her eyes again, they were gone. She had had glimpses of other faces—like Billy. But he was all mixed up with a bale of hay she was trying to drag to the abandoned barn where Irish was hidden. Then the bale of hay turned into Red, with his hair on fire and she couldn't find Irish anywhere. . . .

Rosemary turned her head and saw bouquets of flowers, bowls and vases of them everywhere there was room to put them down. She looked down at her bandaged arms and hands—*what had happened to Irish?*

She had to know! She tried to remember the last few moments at the stables and couldn't. She had put Miss

135

America in the Hitchcock Pen and then the fire truck had come. *And that was all she could remember!*

She didn't have any idea how long she had been in the hospital. What about Red? Was he all right?

How long would she have to wait before someone came in? she wondered. She had so many questions to ask. She looked out the window and decided it must be early in the morning. But what morning? What day was it?

A nurse bustled in with a tray which she put on the stand next to Rosemary's bed and busied herself with paper cups of water and pills and a thermometer.

"How long have I been here?" Rosemary asked.

The nurse jumped. "Good morning, dear. Welcome back."

"Good morning," Rosemary said politely. "Have I been here a week?"

"Mmmhmmm, let's see. . . ." The nurse shook down the thermometer with maddening slowness. "A little more than that."

The thermometer was pushed into Rosemary's mouth and her questions were temporarily stopped. Supposing Irish had been. . . . What had happened to him?

The nurse whisked the thermometer out of Rosemary's mouth, read it, and said, "Well, I see we're better this morning."

"Do you know anything about the fire?" Rosemary asked.

"No, dear. And I don't think you should try to talk too much right at first.

"I know that you were burned and now you're improving. You've had a lot of company who could prob-

136

ably tell you about the fire, but up to now you haven't been ready for them. We'll see if you can't see someone this afternoon."

After giving Rosemary a pill and allowing her a sip of water to wash it down, she prepared to leave. At the door she said archly, "You've had a beau here every afternoon since you came, so I imagine he'll be back today. He's already brought you about three bunches of flowers. He has black curly hair and he's about eight or nine years old. Do you know who I mean?"

Rosemary nodded slowly as the door swung shut noiselessly. Would Billy know?

But Billy wasn't her first visitor that day after all. Mr. Sedgwick and Cindy were. Rosemary felt better as soon as she saw his kind face and warm smile. He would tell her about Irish.

Mr. Sedgwick didn't seem to think she should do too much talking either. He promised to tell her everything he knew, to talk as long as she liked, provided it didn't upset her.

Rosemary thanked him with her eyes. If he didn't want her to talk, she wouldn't, but she begged silently for information about Irish.

As though he read her thoughts, he said, "All of us who could spare the room have taken a horse from Fallow Field. I brought Dublin Jack home the night of the fire."

Rosemary closed her eyes in relief and said a silent prayer of thanks. Mr. Sedgwick was still talking. He'd been called to the phone that night and had hitched his trailer to the station wagon "just in case" when he went to the stables. All the horses were saved but the stables

137

had burned to the ground. Fortunately, there hadn't been a breath of wind and the fire hadn't spread. The paddocks were still standing, the kennels were safe, and so was the house.

The horses that weren't being boarded out were still in the paddocks. Mr. Sedgwick said they were getting rough looking and sunburned, but nobody minded. Everyone was so thankful the horses had been saved. "You can't imagine how much of a heroine you are, Rosemary. There was a story about you in the paper and a picture your uncle gave the reporter."

"And Pete made a special trip down from Echo Lake to see you but you weren't well enough for company," Cindy eagerly added.

"I have a new boy friend," she continued. "He doesn't ride but I think I can get him interested. He's dreamy. He's tall and has black hair and is a wonderful swimmer. He goes to a boarding school in Arizona. I'll tell you about him when you're better."

"You mean there's still *more* to tell?" her father asked in mock astonishment.

Rosemary listened even while her thoughts were on Irish, so close to her uncle's house—right next door, in fact. But Mr. Sedgwick was talking about Mr. Medford now.

". . . and he's going to build a new barn as soon as he gets back next week—a modern, fireproof one. He already has an architect working on the plans."

Rosemary closed her eyes again. For a minute she'd forgotten about Mr. Medford. Now that Irish couldn't be hidden away and forgotten in a dark, closed stall, what would Mr. Medford do with him? She turned her head drearily to the wall and closed her eyes, her visitors almost forgotten. . . .

When she opened them again, she looked straight at Billy. His eyes widened in surprise, causing his glasses to slip down his nose.

"Hi, Rosie! Boy, I'm sure glad you're awake. I get tired of looking at those old bandages. They're on different today than they were yesterday.

"Yesterday they went this way," and he criss-crossed his arms elaborately, "and today they're . . ." he explained with more arm movements. "Boy! I know those bandages by heart.

"Debbie brought me down today. We found out Mr. Sedgwick and Cindy were here and the nurse said you could have only one more company. Tomorrow Debbie and I are going to get here first."

Rosemary smiled as she listened to Billy jump from one subject to another. He pointed out the bouquet the cubbers had sent her, told her about a sissy birthday party he'd been forced to go to and the new horse his father was having shipped out from the east for him.

She asked him about Red and he said vaguely that he was okay and that his dad had suggested that he seek another type of work—in another state.

She must have fallen asleep after that because presently the nurse was shaking her and telling her she wanted to take her temperature.

Now Rosemary could identify each day by name— Wednesday, Thursday, Friday, and Saturday. Then the start of a new week and Mr. Medford would be home. The days seemed to fly and yet they dragged.

She couldn't fight any more. She might just as well

be tied to the bed. She couldn't do anything now except pray that Mr. Medford wouldn't decide that Irish was too badly scarred, or that he didn't want to bother with him.

She remembered what Dr. Potter had said about Mr. Medford, about his having so many businesses and so many interests and projects and so many horses, too. She'd never known anyone like that. If he had so many horses, scattered all over, maybe he wouldn't want to be bothered with one lone brown horse that still needed lots of care.

With a sinking heart she realized that she was going to have to confess the truth to Mr. Medford, that she'd gone against Red's orders and done a lot of things with Irish she wasn't supposed to do. And the most awful of all—planning to steal him. He would know she wasn't to be trusted. He wouldn't want her to work in the new stables. He wouldn't want Billy to take lessons from her. But how was she to begin?

She could forget her worries for a little while when she had company. One afternoon the cubbers visited her with a basket of fruit. Even Don came to see her and Mrs. Hopkins. Cindy always brought presents— horse books and magazines and a book rest to hold them on. Debbie and Anne visited often. Billy showed up every day.

Then it was a new week and all too soon Mr. Medford stood beside her bed, seeming to fill the whole room with his presence.

She wet her lips nervously. How was she to begin?

"Well—the doctor tells me you'll be able to go home in a day or two," Mr. Medford said. "I wish I

140

could have gotten here sooner but I had a few things to take care of first.

"Rosemary, you did a wonderfully brave thing and I want you to know how much I appreciate it—we all do. Until the new barn is finished, which probably won't be until well in the cubbing season, consider you're on a long vacation—with pay."

Rosemary hardly heard him. She would have to make a start. But how?

He was still talking. ". . . everybody's version of the fire except yours. We've figured it out pretty well, except for one thing. What were you doing at the stables at that late hour?"

She wouldn't have to make a start, Rosemary thought with anguish. It was made for her. "I went to the stables . . ." she said in a low voice. She cleared her throat. What would he do to her? Have her arrested? "I was going to steal Irish," she confessed faintly.

"Who?" It sounded like an explosion.

"I mean Dublin Jack."

"You went to the stables to steal that brown horse of mine?" he asked incredulously. "Why?"

It was hopeless. How could she explain? She remained silent.

"Child, I know Red has been responsible for a lot of hanky-panky at the stables. Why don't you start at the beginning and tell me everything?"

It was hard. Mr. Medford wasn't as easy to talk to as Mr. Sedgwick. She started from the very beginning, from the first time she'd seen Irish. She told him everything she'd done—but not about Red hitting the horse with the chain. She never mentioned Red by name,

141

She just said she was afraid something might happen to Irish while Mr. Medford was away.

And then, like a baby, she had to start crying.

"Whoa, now," Mr. Medford said, as he offered her his handkerchief. "I didn't mean to upset you.

"I was going to let you go on a horse-buying expedition, anywhere you want, and find yourself a nice ladies' hunter so you could whip for us when the hunt season starts. But if it's Dublin Jack you want, he's yours, child.

"Rosemary, I have a confession to make, too. I make mistakes, like everyone else. I trusted the opinion of the wrong person on that horse. I see now I made a mistake all the way around. But I haven't entirely lost faith in my own judgment—I didn't do badly when I hired you," and he patted her gently on her bandaged arm. "And that brings me to one other thing I wanted to talk about," he was brushing aside her incoherent thanks. "I can't stay too long," he looked at his watch. "Do you think you feel all right now? I don't want the nurse to bawl me out for upsetting you."

Rosemary smiled radiantly and blew her nose hard. "I'm fine, really. I feel like getting dressed and going home right this minute."

"Well, you know by now that we're going ahead and building new stables. But the house is intact and ready for occupancy. While we were in Ireland, Mrs. Randolph and I found a successor for Red. He'll be the new stable manager and huntsman. He's had years of experience and I guarantee you're going to like him. Would you like to meet him now?"

Rosemary was only vaguely aware of Mr. Medford's

142

question. She had Irish, she had her job, she was going to be a whip. She could see herself hunting Irish when his leg was healed. She would wear a black coat with the hunt colors. She watched herself and Irish galloping down a lane, turning sharply and popping a small chicken coop as hounds streamed over on either side. . . .

Mr. Medford was standing up. He was getting ready to leave. He wasn't looking at her! She hadn't answered his question—what was it—something about meeting the new stable manager. Had he said something besides that? Oh, how rude she'd been!

He had the door open but he wasn't walking through. He was holding it and beckoning someone on the other side. Mrs. Randolph came in with a quick smile for Rosemary and then she, too, looked through the open door.

A strange man walked in hesitantly. But he wasn't a stranger—he was her father!

She must be dreaming. Mr. Medford wasn't really back. She hadn't been given Irish. She'd never be a whip in the hunt and ride over jumps. It was all a sorry dream. Instinctively she pinched herself—hard—and it hurt!

Mrs. Randolph was speaking. "It was the most wonderful thing, Rosemary, that you should tell me about your uncle, that I should remember his name and mention it to Mr. Medford. Rosemary, dear, meet your uncle, Sean O'Connor."

Rosemary looked at the man so like her father, the same curly black hair and blue eyes, the same smile wrinkles around his mouth, the same slightly bowed horseman's legs. Tears started down her cheeks again.

143

Her uncle came forward slowly. "Lass, the last thing we wanted was to make you cry. While we were waitin' for visitin' hours, we went to see your Uncle Ed. A fine, understandin' man, he is. He knows how 'twill be for me and your Aunt Ma-r-r-r-y and the three small cousins you haven't even clapped eyes on yet.

"We'll not be knowin' your ways in this country, Rosie-lass, we need you. When you're well, you're to come and live with us in the cottage at Fallow Field. There, there, little Rosie-posie, don't cry."

Two bandaged arms encircled Uncle Sean as her happy tears soaked his rough tweed coat that smelled just like another coat she'd once known. Rosemary was really home.

Biography of Selma Hudnut

Selma Hudnut became interested in horses at an early age and began reading everything she could on the subject. She learned to ride at the Mills College Riding School, Oakland, California, and soon found that the best way to learn about horses was to "spend a few thousand hours in close proximity to them."

She has only owned four horses but has cared for many others for varying lengths of time. She was the owner of an Army-trained, Olympic prospect named Billy the Kid, who was 11 years old when given to her and performed for her with distinction in hunter and jumper classes for over seven years.

Mrs. Hudnut helped a trail ride association to plan and build their first outside hunter course, taught equitation and coached winners in state-wide competitions, and operated a boarding stable.

She has been a judge in the American Horse Shows Association roster in the division of hunters, jumpers and hunter seat equitation since 1959. She has written for many west coast horse magazines and contributed to *The Chronicle of the Horse,* a weekly horse paper in Virginia revered by all exhibitors of hunters, jumpers, by polo players and pony clubbers. She frequently judges horse shows with her husband and enjoys these, from the county fair type to backyard horse shows which children put on for their friends and families. Her home is in Walnut Creek, California.